This is madne

Tamsin told herself that, as she tried frantically to calm the rapid racing of her heart. But there was no such thing as calm while Ivo was touching her lips, making them tremble with desire. She wanted to kiss his fingers, nibble them, provoke him as he was provoking her. She wanted—oh, it was insane, the things she wanted! Absolutely insane!

We hope you're enjoying our new addition to our Contemporary Romance series—stories which take a light-hearted look at the Zodiac and show that love can be written in the stars!

Every month you can get to know a different combination of star-crossed lovers, with one story that follows the fortunes of a hero or a heroine when they embark on the romance of a lifetime with somebody born under another sign of the Zodiac. This month features a sizzling love-affair between **Aquarius** and **Gemini**.

To find out more fascinating facts about this month's featured star sign, turn to the back pages of this book. . .

ABOUT THIS MONTH'S AUTHOR

Anne Beaumont says: 'The Taurean bull in my star sign must have a very bemused expression on his face. I don't so much plod as leap all over the place, doing everything but what I should be doing. When I *don't* have to do something, that's when I do it. I think it's because I was a very overdue baby. I should have been an Aries!'

THE THREAD OF LOVE

BY
ANNE BEAUMONT

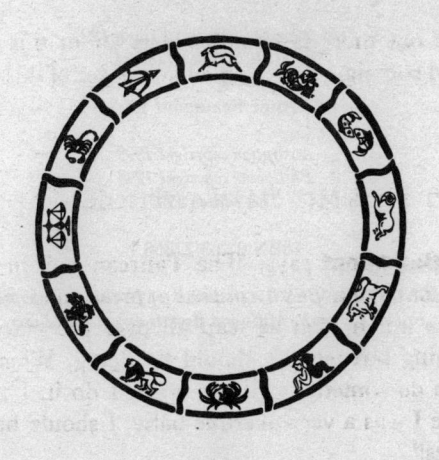

MILLS & BOON LIMITED
ETON HOUSE 18–24 PARADISE ROAD
RICHMOND SURREY TW9 1SR

All the characters in this book have no existence outside the imagination of the Author, and have no relation whatsoever to anyone bearing the same name or names. They are not even distantly inspired by any individual known or unknown to the Author, and all the incidents are pure invention.

All Rights Reserved. The text of this publication or any part thereof may not be reproduced or transmitted in any form or by any means, electronic or mechanical, including photocopying, recording, storage in an information retrieval system, or otherwise, without the written permission of the publisher.

This book is sold subject to the condition that it shall not, by way of trade or otherwise, be lent, resold, hired out or otherwise circulated without the prior consent of the publisher in any form of binding or cover other than that in which it is published and without a similar condition including this condition being imposed on the subsequent purchaser.

First published in Great Britain 1993 by Mills & Boon Limited

© Anne Beaumont 1993

*Australian copyright 1993
Philippine copyright 1993
This edition 1993*

ISBN 0 263 77868 1

STARSIGN ROMANCES is a trademark of Harlequin Enterprises B.V., Fribourg Branch. Mills and Boon is an authorised user.

*Set in 10 on 12 pt Linotron Baskerville
01-9301-54011 Z*

*Typeset in Great Britain by Centracet, Cambridge
Made and printed in Great Britain*

CHAPTER ONE

DAVID's feather-light kisses traced the line of her jaw and continued their sensuous journey of exploration downwards until he found the throbbing nerve where her neck joined her shoulder. Maria sighed and winced in the most delicious torment, and the pressure of his lips increased demandingly.

She was his, she knew that now, but was he hers? That was the question that was tantalising her mind as much as his lips were tantalising her body. She had to find the answer to it, and soon—so soon!—or it would be too late...

So what *was* the answer?

Damned if I know, Tamsin thought despairingly, reading over the scribbled opening lines of her latest short story and tossing her notebook aside with a sigh of exasperation. Even now, when she was propped up comfortably in bed, with a gale lashing the windows to create lots of lovely atmosphere, the story wouldn't come right.

She wasn't having any problems with Maria, her heroine. But her hero was another matter. He just wouldn't behave! He was supposed to be fair-haired and blue-eyed and gentlemanly, but since she'd arrived at this isolated house in the wilds of Suffolk he'd transformed himself into a dark-haired man with come-to-bed eyes and kisses that scorched her skin even when they were only imaginary. A predatory male if ever there was one!

'And I don't like predatory males,' Tamsin said aloud, hoping her indignant words would chase away the dark-haired man, stop him taking over her story and wrecking it. 'Do you hear me? I don't like you! I know your type too well. You grab first and ask questions later—if you stick around long enough for there to be a later, which is highly doubtful. Get out of my story and get out of my head!'

Feeling a bit better for her outburst, but not a lot, Tamsin settled back against the banked-up pillows and chewed the end of her pen as she tried to figure out how the dark-haired man had got into her head in the first place.

She didn't know him, she was sure of that, and yet he had such a distinctive face that she almost recognised him. Oh, if only she could recall from where! She couldn't, though, and that was what was so frustrating.

It was so unusual, too, since she was good at puzzles of any kind. Her free-wheeling brain was also capable of taking great leaps into fantasy and making sense of things that were incomprehensible to other people, but not this time!

In fact, the only thing she was sure of was that in some peculiar way the dark-haired man seemed to come with this strange house. She certainly hadn't been bothered by him before she'd arrived here this afternoon.

'Except, of course,' she puzzled aloud, 'that there's no man in this house. There isn't anybody at all. Only me.'

Now was that a puzzle, or was that a puzzle? No wonder frustration was stifling her creative flow. In the end, though, there was nothing she could do but admit defeat and give up trying to solve it. Gritting her teeth in exasperation, Tamsin reached again for her notepad and concentrated hard, determined to work her way back into a more positive frame of mind and salvage her story.

Almost immediately the dark-haired man thrust his smiling face between her and the lines she'd written. It was a very mocking smile he had, and his mockery was directed straight at her.

You need to meet me, he seemed to be saying. You need to live the story. Then, and only then, will you be able to write it.

For a moment Tamsin was as shocked as if he'd actually spoken. Then reaction set in and she laughed at her own folly. When characters started talking back—especially an unwanted character with a face no more than on the craggy side of handsome—it was time to shut down her vivid imagination and call it a day. Or, rather, a night. . .

Once more she tossed aside her notepad, not caring when it slipped from the bedside table and into the waste-paper basket. The way she was feeling at the moment, that was the right place for it.

Exhaustion was propably her trouble, she consoled herself. She'd only got back from researching the background for her story in Corfu this morning, then she'd been more or less blackmailed into coming up here before she'd had time to unpack her bags, with no opportunity all day for a proper meal, and finally she'd been too keen to get on with her story to bother cooking for herself when she'd at last had the chance.

Heaven only knew where the dark-haired man fitted into all that, but Tamsin was sure he'd be gone in the morning when she'd had a good sleep and got her head back together.

Yawning, she slipped of her watch, set the alarm on it for seven in the morning and clicked off the bedside lamp. Just as she was settling down to sleep, the gale hurled itself with fresh fury against the rattling windowpanes.

Tamsin retreated hurriedly under the duvet, all the spooky novels she'd ever read chasing through her mind, reminding her of how very alone she was. Sometimes it wasn't a good thing to have an imagination as vivid as hers...

'Definitely time to sleep,' she murmured to herself, snuggling deep into the feather pillows and pulling the duvet up over her head. For a few minutes, though, a niggle of worry kept her wakeful.

The romantic stories she wrote were so popular that she was already ranked among the most successful of the young, up-and-coming authors—but the story she was writing at the moment was a special commission and it had a deadline on it.

Come hell or high water, it had to be finished by next Monday. And it's Tuesday already, Tamsin thought drowsily, annoyed that if it hadn't been for the intrusion of the dark-haired man she'd probably have got most of it roughed out tonight.

She was still fretting about it when she slipped over the borderline between wakefulness and sleep, and she slept soundly for almost an hour. She should have slept soundly all night, but suddenly she was awake again, certain that an unusual noise had aroused her, and her nerves quivered as she sought to identify it.

She heard nothing more ominous than screaming wind and running water and, reassured, she reached out and switched on the bedside lamp. The light that bathed the room showed that everything was just as it should be.

Her nerves stopped jumping, and Tamsin blamed the gale for waking her. This house was in a rural area, much too isolated to be bothered by chance prowlers. Besides, nobody in their right mind would venture out on a night like this.

Tamsin switched off the light, then thought, Nobody in their right mind... Dear God, was there a maniac loose in the house?

No, of course there wasn't! she scolded herself. Whatever would she be imagining next? Then she realised that the running water she'd heard when she'd first awoken wasn't rain. It was coming from inside the house!

Now steady on, she told herself. Some tiles must have come off the roof, that was all. A nuisance, sure, but the worst she had to do was go downstairs and find some buckets to catch the leaks. Drat! Still, the house was centrally heated. If she was about to be swept away on a tidal flood, at least she wouldn't freeze to death first.

Feeling better now that her sense of humour had reasserted itself, Tamsin was reaching once more for the bedside lamp when her eyes turned towards the darkened door. There was a light showing under it. Somebody *was* in the house!

Fear surged up again, but this time she was awake enough to react more reasonably. She had to arm herself and go out there to discover who it was. And to think that when her sister Gemma had begged her help in looking after this house for twenty-four hours she'd sworn it would be a doddle!

Swallowing hard, Tamsin wished she were more used to this sort of work as she pushed back the duvet and swung her silk-pyjamaed legs out of bed. She went down on her knees, stealthily unplugged the brass bedside lamp and grasped it as a makeshift weapon.

But what on earth was the intruder running all that water for? It sounded as though he was having a shower. Intruders weren't that fastidious, were they?

Tamsin shivered, then she almost collapsed with relief as a far more rational explanation occurred to her. Mrs Durand, who owned this house and had appealed to Gemma's agency for somebody to look after things while she was away—it had to be her out there. She must have hit some snag on her emergency journey north, the gale perhaps, and been forced back home.

Tamsin went weak with reaction but, just in case, she clutched the brass lamp militantly as she crept outside her bedroom and peered along the passage. Not that she could see much. For one thing, her long fair hair was in her eyes, and, for another, the panelled passage was full of the twists and turns that were typical of an ancient house that had been altered and added on to down through the years.

The water was still running, though. Pushing her heavy hair back over her shoulders, Tamsin crept silently towards the sound, her belief that Mrs Durand had returned strengthening with each step. There was no doubt about it; she was moving away from the guest rooms and into the family wing of the house.

This was pretty much unknown territory to her, but just as she reached one of the family bathrooms the sound of running water ceased. Moments later the bathroom door opened, then a shock like a bolt from the blue whooshed the air out of her lungs. Confronting her wasn't the sweet and slender Mrs Durand but a tall, muscular man, naked save for a towel wrapped around his waist.

Water still dripped from his dark wavy hair, but it was neither his near-nakedness nor his threatening physical presence that turned Tamsin to jelly: it was his face. It was on the craggy side of handsome, lit with come-to-bed brown eyes, and distinguished by a cleft carved deeply into his forceful chin.

Apparently his need for a shower hadn't stretched as far as a need for a shave. There was dark stubble on his chin. Tamsin didn't recognise the stubble but she recognised everything else about him.

Here, solid, assured and exuding an urgent, raw-nerved sensuality that smote her like a physical force, was the phantom dark-haired man who'd stamped himself on her subconscious and wrecked her short story.

It wasn't possible. It simply wasn't possible. Tamsin stared, aghast, at him, unable to believe what her own eyes were seeing. It was all too much. There was a roaring noise in her ears, everything went black and the lamp fell from her hand. Ignominiously she fell in a senseless, crumpled heap at his large and naked feet...

Tamsin had no idea what had happened to her when her eyes opened again, but the first thing she saw was the dark-haired man's face looming over her. It was close, much too close, and his hands were undoing the expensive silk-covered buttons of her pyjama jacket. She could feel his strong fingers warm against her throat as one button gave, and then another.

She screamed and began to fight, raining frantic blows against his face and the unyielding muscles of his chest, her legs flailing wildly as she twisted her body in a desperate attempt to break free of him.

'That's all I need,' he snapped in a deep voice that rasped the edges of her already shattered nerves.

Tamsin felt the full force of his powerful arms as he pinned her down by the shoulders and held her in a merciless grip as she strained to wriggle free. It was a hopeless struggle, and when she finally collapsed, panting and spent, she stared wildly into the dark eyes that her imagination had somehow conjured up and therefore couldn't possibly be real.

She moaned and turned her head away, waiting for the nightmare to recede and blessed reality to return. It was only then that she realised she was on a bed, not her safe single bed in the guest room, but a big one in a room she'd never seen before.

At the same time she realised that this was no nightmare. The dark eyes burning into hers were as real as the big hands bruising her soft flesh.

'Who are you?' she gasped. 'Who the devil are you?'

'Who the devil are *you*?' he snarled back. 'I come home and——'

'Home!' Tamsin broke in, outrage overcoming her fear. 'This isn't your home. This is Mrs Durand's home, and she lives alone.'

'So you know that much, do you?' he said with a contempt that would have flicked Tamsin to the raw if she hadn't been so frightened and outraged.

'Of course I know that much!' she exclaimed indignantly. 'I'm Mrs Durand's house-sitter.'

'Her *what*?'

'House-sitter,' Tamsin repeated, thinking he must be a real beast to bellow at her like that. If he had the slightest scrap of compassion he'd realise he was overpowering enough without that.

'What in the blazes is a house-sitter?' he demanded irately.

'I really don't see what it is to do with you,' she retorted, trying to hide her fear behind a travesty of dignity. 'You break in here, you assault me——'

'The hell I have. You fainted at my feet.'

Contempt was still written all over his face and it was beginning to rankle, but not half as much as what he'd said. A hot denial sprang to her lips and she exclaimed, 'I never faint!'

'Then you give a pretty good imitation. How do you think you got on this bed? Because I carried you here——'

'To rape me!' Tamsin accused wildly. 'You were undressing me when I woke up. What did you do to make me pass out like that? Hit me on the head?'

Cold eyes bored into hers and he said witheringly, 'No, but I'll bear it in mind if you don't stop being hysterical.'

'I'm not hysterical!' Even as Tamsin denied it, the high pitch of her voice confirmed that she was far from being in control—of herself, the situation, everything. How awful, and how unlike herself.

Ashamed, she took a deep breath and said with forced calmness, 'Well, if I am, it's hardly surprising.' Then, trying hard not to be intimidated by his strength and his all-too-physical aura, she added with only the slightest quiver in her voice, 'Now, perhaps you wouldn't mind letting me go.'

His grip eased slightly, but he still held her down as he demanded, 'How do I know you won't try to claw my eyes out again?'

'How do I know you won't try to assault me again?'

'I haven't assaulted you.' He glared irritably at her but he let her go.

'Yes, you have, and I'm sure I've got the bruises to prove it. My shoulders feel black and blue.'

'However you feel, the fact is that you fainted,' he told her brusquely. 'I carried you in here and loosened your buttons so that you could breathe more easily. It seemed the right thing to do at the time but you started lashing out as though I were Jack the Ripper, so if you're bruised it's your own fault. I had to hold you down. Those claws of yours are lethal.'

He sounded as though he was telling the truth. Tamsin still eyed him warily, though, as she sat up and hastily rebuttoned her pyjama jacket.

She felt uncomfortable at having a near-naked man so close to her, and she felt distinctly threatened when he sat on the bed next to her, although for some reason she didn't have time to go into her instincts told her the immediate danger had passed.

What was she supposed to do to stay out of danger, though? Keep him talking, of course; try to establish some sort of rapport between them. That was what women were supposed to do in this sort of situation, weren't they? Tamsin searched her mind frantically for some topic of conversation that might pacify him, but self-disgust made her exclaim, 'I still can't believe I did anything as puerile as fainting!'

'Neither can I,' he responded unhelpfully. 'I thought females gave up that sort of thing when they gave up tight corsets, and you're definitely not wearing one of those.'

Tamsin glared at him. His words reminded her vividly of the raw sensuality she'd felt when she'd first seen him, and of the imprints she could still feel of his strong fingers on her tender body. Why, oh, why did he have to be so *physical* about everything? It was having a funny effect on her, making her feel physical, too, and she wasn't that sort of person. Especially with a stranger!

There was no denying, though, that the almost clinical way he was studying her was making her as conscious of her body as she was of his. Embarrassed, she blushed hotly, then she hated herself for blushing as much as she hated herself for fainting.

It was difficult not to blush, though, when the silk of her pyjamas suddenly seemed little more than a second skin, and this man who was so close didn't seem to have noticed that the towel wrapped around his waist had slipped to his lithe hips.

Her subconscious might know his face well, but it hadn't got around to putting a body to it. She hadn't bargained on such a dark mat of hair on his chest, and such magnificent fitness. She was disturbingly aware of the way his muscles rippled every time he moved, too, but she couldn't very well avert her eyes. She had to watch him in case he became violent and pounced on her again.

'What's your name?' he asked abruptly, his clinical appraisal of her apparently over. 'Or do you prefer fainting all over the place to introducing yourself properly?'

His sarcasm and the satirical quirk of his dark eyebrows annoyed Tamsin so intensely that she forgot to be cautious, and flared, 'I don't faint all over the place, and my name is Tamsin Sinclair. Is there anything else you want to know?'

He was quite unmoved by her little burst of temper

and replied calmly, 'Yes. What's a house-sitter? Some kind of double talk for a squatter?'

'No, it isn't! A house-sitter looks after other people's houses while they're away.' For a moment Tamsin considered telling him that she wasn't a regular house-sitter, but she decided that would only complicate the situation even more.

Once again his eyebrows took on a satirical slant. 'Considering the state of your nerves, living in strange houses must mean you do an awful lot of fainting. You don't strike me as being capable of looking after yourself, let alone anything else.'

'I've never fainted in my life before! It was just that—that...' Tamsin broke off in dismay. Damn! There was no way she could explain the traumatic effect his face had had on her, not without him thinking she was totally gaga...

Swallowing her chagrin, she continued lamely, 'It must have been the storm that spooked me, that and being overtired. I only arrived this afternoon, you see, and Mrs Durand had to shoot off to Cumberland right away. I don't think any woman can be blamed for being unnerved, anyway, if she wakes up to find a man has forced his way into the house.'

'Except that I didn't force my way in.'

'You must have!' Tamsin contradicted. 'I checked the doors were bolted as well as locked before I went to bed.'

'There's no bolt on the french windows in the sitting-room, and I have a key,' he told her sardonically.

'A key!' Tamsin stared at him in disbelief. 'Mrs Durand didn't say anything about anybody having a key. She should have, if strange men are going to wander in and take showers in the middle of the night without so much as a by-your-leave.'

Unexpectedly he smiled, then explained, 'She wasn't expecting me.'

'Do you think I was?' she answered wrathfully, although at the same time she wished he hadn't smiled. It made him look so different. Not half so sardonic, but approachable. Even nice...

Worse, it was the sort of smile that made her want to smile back, but she mustn't. He might think she was leading him on, encouraging him to—to——!

Tamsin's thoughts failed her, and with something like wonder she pondered why she hadn't been off this bed and fleeing into the night ages ago. True, she'd decided it was safer to keep him talking, and true, the sheer height and breadth of him made an intimidating barricade between herself and the door, but that scarcely explained why they were sitting here chatting as though she were used to entertaining house-breakers in the middle of the night.

Except that he claimed he wasn't one, although that was still to be proved. Whipping up what she saw as a very justifiable sense of outrage, Tamsin accused, 'You insisted I told you my name but you haven't introduced yourself. In fact, you've been very careful not to let me find out who you are.'

'I've been more interested in finding out about you. Blondes have that effect on me. Do you mind?'

'Of course I mind!' She did, too, because he made it sound as though he chatted up blondes as an ongoing hobby. For some peculiar reason, that peeved her very much. It made her feel she wasn't distinctive at all. How could she be, lumped in the plural like that?

'Why do you mind?'

He shot the question at her like a bullet, but she ducked it.

'What I mind is not knowing who you are. You could be a homicidal maniac for all I know.'

'Except that you're not dead.' He was smiling at her again, and Tamsin had the feeling that in other circumstances he could be considerably charming, but that only made her warier of him than ever.

'No, I'm not dead,' she agreed slowly, 'but I still don't know who you are and what you're doing here.'

'My name is Ivo and Mrs Durand is my mother.'

So that was it! Tamsin's relief was short-lived, though, as for some reason his very name quivered sensuously along her overstrung nerves. She was exasperated with herself, and wondered how she'd lost her ability to distance herself from uncomfortable emotions. Normally she could, but not with this man. He was different, somehow. He got through to her.

Once before—and she'd vowed it would only ever be once!—she'd stopped being aloof, and the experience had very nearly destroyed her. Oh, not physically, but mentally, emotionally and spiritually. A year later she was still sort of convalescing, still twice as fragile as she should be and therefore masquerading as twice as tough.

'*Ivo* . . .' she repeated, she didn't know why, and then she was so disconcerted at the sudden hardening of his eyes that she went on rapidly, 'Well, that explains a lot, but it doesn't explain why you arrived in the middle of the night and had a shower.'

'I'm London-based, I'm abroad a lot, and I'm not a nine-till-five man wherever I happen to be. I grab what chances I can to visit my mother. She doesn't mind what time of the day or night I arrive, even if you do, Little Miss House-Sitter.'

Tamsin clenched her teeth at his sarcasm but bit back a retort as he went on, 'And I always shower before I go to bed if I happen to be somewhere civilised enough to have a bathroom. Satisfied?'

He was making her feel foolish now, and all her suppressed emotions boiled over, making her exclaim impetuously, 'No, I'm not satisfied, and I won't be until I find out why I know you!'

She wished fervently that she hadn't said that, but it was too late now. She bit her lip as Ivo eyed her up and down in an insultingly intimate way, then said with cold finality, 'You don't know me. If we'd met before, I'd have remembered—even if you hadn't been wearing sexy silk pyjamas at the time.'

Anger burned through Tamsin at the way he reduced everything to the physical level he so clearly relished, but she was twice as angry with herself for speaking so unguardedly. Now look what she'd got herself into! She couldn't possibly explain to this unashamedly sensual man that the hero of her story kept turning into him. 'I—er—I—er——' she stuttered.

'Yes?' he prompted. 'You—er—what?'

Tamsin ignored his mockery and confessed to only as much as she had to. 'When I first saw you your face seemed familiar. Somehow it—it—seemed to go with the house. I'll admit that sounds crazy but—but——'

'Maybe you saw my photograph in the sitting-room. My mother keeps one on the mantelpiece,' he said, bafflingly cynical again, but Tamsin was preoccupied in recalling what the sitting-room looked like. She'd only looked in there briefly when his mother had hurriedly shown her the main rooms in the house before rushing off.

For the life of her, Tamsin couldn't consciously

remember noticing his photograph among the other family shots, but her subconscious—or her writer's mind—must have registered his likeness and thrown it back at her when she'd been trying to get her story down.

'Mystery solved,' she breathed thankfully, then became aware that his cynicism had deepened into a look that bordered on disbelief. A puzzled frown creased her smooth forehead, and she asked, 'Is something wrong?'

'Apparently not,' he replied, and seemed to be making a conscious effort to relax again.

More puzzled than ever, Tamsin rapidly concluded that Ivo was as complicated as he was physical. His moods were like quicksilver, shifting all the time, but then she was overwhelmed by a new discovery: she was no longer thinking of him as a stranger; she was thinking of him as Ivo, and that was enough to give her—well, a warm feeling.

Before she could come to terms with that, he must have interpreted correctly the confused emotions flitting across her face because he smiled at her again, and instantly her warm feeling smouldered to more intense heat.

Tamsin couldn't believe it, and her wondering lips parted in disbelief. Never, ever before had she reacted this fast and this positively to a man. It was almost as though some strange alchemy was taking place between them.

Stop being so ridiculous, she told herself sharply, knowing full well that this sort of thing only happened in her dreams—those idyllic dreams she kept buried deep within her because so far her experiences with men had only ridiculed them. Especially her disastrous affair with Simeon...

Thinking of Simeon should have brought her swiftly down to earth, but it didn't. The alchemy between her and Ivo was still there, she was sure of it. If she'd been less confused she'd have been shrewd enough to keep it to herself, but her usual judgement deserted her and she blurted out, 'You're not a Gemini, are you?'

For a second, Ivo looked at her as though she was raving. Then his eyebrows took on the satirical slant she was becoming accustomed to, and he said, 'I don't know whether you're a bit of a weirdo or whether you're living on another planet altogether—but yes, I do happen to be a Gemini. What the hell does it matter?'

'It doesn't,' Tamsin denied hastily, regretting her rashness and feeling all kinds of a fool. But it did matter because she was an Aquarian, and the short story she was writing was all about an Aquarian heroine and a Gemini hero!

It was the craziest thing, but it was almost as if real life was echoing her story, and that sort of thing had never happened to her before. She experienced things first, then wrote about them—not the other way around...

Ivo looked carefully at Tamsin's dismayed expression, and said bluntly, 'You're lying. In some screwball sort of way, I think it matters a lot to you that I'm a Gemini.'

'Lying is a rotten thing to accuse me of,' she bluffed, trying too late to cloak her emotions with her usual reserve. 'Do I look like a liar to you?'

Ivo's eyes narrowed, causing an inexplicable increase in Tamsin's pulse-rate. She couldn't understand why, in such a short time, she'd become so extraordinarily sensitive to his changes of mood. Yet there was no denying that the throb in his voice seemed to enter her heart as he replied, 'If I told you exactly what you look like to me right now you'd accuse me again of wanting to ravish you. Not that I don't, although I do expect the right degree of co-operation.'

Her lips widened in an 'Oh' of astonishment, and Ivo reached out to trace their parted outline with a lazily tantalising finger, his voice deepening further as he went on, 'But you're more than ready to co-operate, aren't you, Tamsin?'

Her lips quivered responsively to his sensuous touch, triggering off an alien and far more dangerous reaction deep within her. She was so bewildered that it was a few moments before she could force herself to respond to the alarm bells ringing in her head.

'No,' she gasped belatedly, wriggling as far away from him as she could until she was crammed up against the bedhead. She grabbed the loose end of the duvet from the far side of the bed and pulled it up to her shoulders like a protective shield. 'No. . .no, I'm not. In fact, I'm not interested in physical relationships at all. I'm—I'm just not a physical sort of person. . .'

'The hell you're not,' he said, sudden, inexplicable anger roughening his voice. 'I can take a straight no if I have to, but you're lying again and I can't stand being lied to. Especially when I've been deliberately led on.'

'I'm not lying and I haven't led you on!' she cried, wondering how on earth he'd got that idea.

With something between a snarl and a challenge, Ivo retorted, 'No? Then let's put it to the test.'

He took her by the shoulders and gave her a sudden jerk that precipitated her into his arms. She felt her soft, full breasts crush against his hard matted chest and her head fell back, her hair spreading its silky cascade over his shoulder.

For a shocked second she scarcely realised what was happening, then she found herself looking up into his stormy face. Excitement seared through her, a delicious, treacherous excitement that ran out of control until she read the naked intent burning in his dark eyes.

CHAPTER TWO

TAMSIN was aware that somehow a terrible misunderstanding had cropped up between them, but there was no time to go into that now. She felt a weakening desire to feel—just for a second!—the touch of his firm lips on hers before she protested, but lust for its own sake was what she most abhorred, and so she cried out, 'No, don't! Let me go!'

Ivo paused, searching her eyes. Their lips were so close, the tension throbbing so palpably between them that is seemed to rob the atmosphere of air, making her gasp for breath.

'No,' she repeated, but so weakly that the sound was lost in their ragged breathing. She swallowed and tried harder. 'Ivo, no!'

With a smothered curse he released her and she scrambled back to the top of the bed, trembling fingers clutching at the duvet to cover herself again, and flinching when he said contemptuously, 'It's a bit late to be coy.'

'I don't know what you mean,' she faltered. 'I don't know why you think I'm lying, why you think I'm leading you on or—or anything. None of it makes any sense to me.'

'Oh, come off it!' he said harshly. 'You don't really think I believed that cock and bull story about you not knowing who I am? All right, so I played along with you for a while. That was because I *wanted* to believe you—God knows why!—but, if you didn't recognise my face the moment you saw it, you certainly recognised my name.'

Tamsin shook her head in mute denial, and that seemed to goad him to fresh fury.

'Stop playing the little innocent,' he thundered. 'I saw the look in your eyes when I introduced myself. I could hardly miss it, I've seen it so many times before. If you think I'm flattered that a reputation like mine has girls like you doing anything to be added to the list, you're way out. It sickens me...especially when it comes to girls who are just after a vicarious thrill and panic when their bluff is called.'

Tamsin's bewilderment deepened into a confusion so total that, although she opened her mouth to deny his accusations, not a sound came out.

Ivo stood up, tightened the towel around his hips, and stared mercilessly down at her as he stepped away from the bed. Then he said scornfully, 'Your bluff has been well and truly called.'

Tamsin wished she could think straight, but she was too scorched by his touch, his fury, and the injustice of his accusations riveted her to the spot.

She shook her dishevelled hair back from her face so that she could see him more clearly, and stuttered indignantly, 'I wasn't b-bluffing, or leading you on. If I stayed here longer than I should it was because I really believed you were a house-breaker and th-thought that I had to humour you. By the time I realised you were no such thing, there was so much to explain that I forgot how I was d-dressed and——'

'Stop babbling and get out of here,' he stormed.

'If I'm babbling it's because you're raving!' she flared. 'What sort of a reputation are you on about? Who are you supposed to be and why am I supposed to recognise your name?' Even as she asked the question, her mind cleared and coupled his surname with his Christian name for the first time.

Ivo Durand.

'Oh, my God,' she breathed, appalled, and had to repeat the name to really believe it. 'Ivo Durand...the top society photographer. How could I have been so stupid as not to have made the connection before?'

'How, indeed?' he asked disbelievingly.

'And the top society stud,' she added with revulsion. 'A titled lady seduced away from her husband here, a top model seduced there, and so on and so on. Oh, I know what you're on about now. I've read enough about your scandalous affairs, and so has the rest of the world, but if you think I've ambitions to be your latest conquest, you're way out.'

Tamsin, suddenly remembering where she was, scrambled out of Ivo's bed, drew herself up to her full five feet eight inches of height and continued scathingly, 'I'm sorry I was so slow on the uptake, but blame that on the unusual way we met. Now that I know exactly who you are, I'm only too glad to get out of your room—and if you stray into mine I promise that the next place I drop that brass lamp will be right on your head.'

Ivo clapped his hands in slow applause. 'A great performance, good enough to fool anybody but me,' he said mockingly. 'The trouble is, I know your sort of woman, Tamsin Sinclair. You're a tease, a would-be temptress who can't resist the challenge of a man with a reputation for being dangerous—but you haven't the nerve to go through with what you've started.'

Tamsin retorted icily, 'You don't know anything about my sort of woman, Ivo Durand, and nothing at all about me in particular. I'd rather have a bug in my bed than a two-legged bedhopper who thinks he's God's gift to women. I loathe men without morals, a sense of responsibility or any notion of constancy. Do your hear me? *Loathe*!'

There was a little silence while they glared at each other, then Ivo's expression changed. His stormy look vanished and he drawled, 'That's a pity, because I'm just beginning to get interested in you. I probably need my head examined, but I'm damned if I don't believe you—almost. Probably,' he added thoughtfully, 'because there's nothing like a bit of novelty to tempt a jaded palate.'

Tamsin gasped, but as he began to walk leisurely towards her she lost a little of her poise and backed away. 'You haven't been listening to me,' she objected, uncomfortably breathless again. 'I couldn't have made it clearer that whatever interests you doesn't interest me!'

'Oh, I got the message, but there are so many other things you have to make clear. Are you sleepy?'

His question was so unexpected that Tamsin was caught off guard and admitted involuntarily, 'No.' She was surprised to find that she meant it, too, and put that down to Ivo's arrogance incensing her so much that she'd forgotten all about her exhaustion.

'Neither am I,' he replied. 'Get your dressing-gown and meet me downstairs for coffee. Then you can tell me in less enticing circumstances all the things I suddenly find myself wanting to know about you. Including,' he added as an afterthought, 'why you want me to be a Gemini.'

'I don't want you to be a Gemini,' she denied quickly, wondering how he could remember that impulsive outburst of hers when so much else had happened since.

'All right, you can tell me why you *don't* want me to be a Gemini.'

Tamsin bit her lip. She knew she was too wide awake now to hope to get to sleep, but the last thing she wanted to do was talk about something that was safer kept to herself. 'It's the middle of the night. Why don't we just go to bed?' she suggested hopefully. 'We can talk things over in the morning.'

Ivo's eyebrows took on the satirical quirk that she'd already learned boded no good for her. 'Now that's what I call the right degree of co-operation,' he murmured.

Instantly she fired up. 'You know darned well I don't mean together!'

'I'm not entirely convinced that what you say is what you mean, although for the moment I'll give you the benefit of the doubt—but out of my room you go. Now!'

He scooped her up into his arms and swung her towards the door. Before she had time to protest, the warmth of his bare arms mocked the slender protection of her silk pyjamas and fused with the warmth of her own body.

It was a very disconcerting sensation and, however much she might be mentally against any contact with him, physically her soft flesh responded to his with welcoming pleasure. She felt almost—thwarted—when he set her firmly down on her feet.

It was such an uncharacteristic reaction that she was shocked, too shocked even to disguise her reaction. Ivo saw her expression and said, 'Yes, I think that's what's called too close for comfort.'

The accuracy with which he'd read her emotions caused a blush to rise painfully from her neck to her face. Ivo watched the tell-tale colour spreading across her cheeks and added softly, 'You and I—too close—are a lethal combination, and whatever you say, Tamsin, you know it as well as I do. Now go and get that dressing-gown.'

Tamsin tried to regain her shattered equilibrium, and her dignity with it, by telling him loftily, 'You could ask, you know. There's no need to boss me around.'

'Oh, but there is, because if you stay around much longer in those seductive scraps of red silk I might change my mind about giving you the benefit of the doubt,' he replied bluntly.

'They're not scraps,' she protested, but Ivo's eyebrows were lowering uncompromisingly. She was weighing up the significance of that when he made it obvious by moving closer to her—and he was close enough already. Another inch and she'd be in his arms.

'I wish,' she began, indignant enough to speak the whole unvarnished truth, 'you'd stop being so physical.'

'You don't wish any such thing,' he contradicted her. 'You only think you do.'

His arrogance got right under Tamsin's skin. She opened her mouth to argue, saw the look in his eyes, and thought better of it. It left her with nothing to do but turn and stalk away from him, burning with all sorts of emotion, of which indignation was only one.

She returned to her room in as much of a turmoil as she'd crept out of it, although of an entirely different kind, because it was dawning on her that Ivo had the ability to disturb her so deeply that her normal knack of switching off uncomfortable emotions wasn't working. Somehow or other, her trip-switch seemed to have passed from her control to his. And she had to get it back.

How?

Calm down was the obvious answer, but, with Ivo's nerve-racking presence just a few doors away, it wasn't easy. Desperately Tamsin tried to convince herself that she was only over-reacting to Ivo's unashamed masculinity because she felt threatened by it, and all she had to do to regain her equilibrium was to refuse to be threatened.

It seemed a tall order, but she should be equal to it. After all, she'd survived her first encounter with him more or less intact, so she must be doing something right, and now she knew exactly what kind of a man she was dealing with. She'd meant it, too, when she'd told him she loathed his lifestyle and wanted no part of it. That should fortify her if all else failed.

Then, out of the blue, she remembered the subconscious image she'd had of Ivo before she'd actually met him, and how everything that was intuitive about her had interpreted his mocking smile to mean: You need to meet me. You need to live the story. Then, and only then, will you be able to write it.

Goosey fingers of *déjà vu* traced icy imprints up and down Tamsin's spine, but for some peculiar reason she was as much excited as frightened. That, obviously, was something to do with his uncanny ability to heighten all her senses. Well, there was only one answer to that. Play it safe!

With that in mind, Tamsin decided that if Ivo regarded her pyjamas as nothing but seductive scraps he might think the same about the slit-sided red silk dressing-gown that went with it. Best to be less provocative altogether!

She stripped off and quickly re-dressed in a multicoloured designer sweater that made her a shapeless mass of chunky wool from neck to hips, and teamed it with tailored jeans that bore startling multicoloured designer patches over areas that were neither frayed nor worn.

Any signals Ivo picked up from her now couldn't possibly be encouraging, she thought with satisfaction. All the same, there was a trace of anxiety in her eyes as she studied her reflection in the dressing-table mirror. She'd realised long ago that her face was a problem for a girl like her, who didn't like to be swept off her feet but needed time to develop her relationships slowly.

It was her full lips that were the trouble, adding blatant sexuality to features that would otherwise be classically chaste: straight nose, dark-fringed blue eyes, finely curved eyebrows and delicately coloured cheeks enhancing a fair complexion. Men might be content to worship from afar a face like hers, if only those provocative lips wouldn't lure them in for plunder!

Tamsin sighed, then suddenly frowned more deeply still. She hadn't studied herself really closely for a long time, but it seemed to her there was a subtle difference in the face reflected back at her. Not so much a difference, perhaps, as a glow that made her eyes look more luminuous, her lips even more outrageously sensual.

Ivo's influence? She didn't want to think so, and she brushed her long hair swiftly, tied it back at the nape of her neck and went over to the bedside table to pick up her watch. Nearly midnight, she saw, and here she was, glowing as though the day were just beginning instead of ending.

She must be out of her mind to be going downstairs for coffee with Ivo at this hour, not that he'd given her any option! If she tried to avoid him by jumping into bed he was quite capable of dragging her out again or, worse, bringing the coffee up to her room for an even cosier tête-à-tête. Whichever way she looked at it, joining him voluntarily was the lesser choice of evils.

The smell of percolating coffee warned her that he was already in the kitchen long before she reached the big, mellow room with its beamed ceiling, oak cupboards and dressers, and time-worn ladder-backed chairs surrounding a huge scrubbed table.

What she wasn't prepared for was the look Ivo threw her. It summed her up immediately and told her he was amused by her defensive clothes. 'You forgot your wellington boots,' he said mockingly. 'You even forgot your slippers. Has any man ever told you that you have beautiful feet?'

Tamsin was startled. Of course no man had ever told her any such thing! Beautiful everything else, maybe, but definitely not feet. In fact, it was hard to think of a man whose physical interest in her hadn't started at her mouth and ended at her hips, with the rest of her being disappointedly discarded—from her point of view—as irrelevant.

Involuntarily, though, she followed Ivo's eyes and found herself watching her bare toes curling under themselves in embarrassment at being the focal point of attention.

Trust me to have forgotten my slippers, she thought. There was no use pleading she'd been too busy thinking about other things when she'd changed, otherwise Ivo was bound to ask what sort of things. He'd already proved what an alarming habit he had of latching on to the last thing she wanted to discuss.

She shot a surreptitious look at him and was surprised to see he was wearing well-worn jeans, a plain black T-shirt, and soft suede moccasins. She was glad he wasn't watching her face, and once more she followed his gaze back to her feet, thinking flusteredly that they couldn't both go on staring at her pink toes, still curling under with embarrassment.

'They're cold,' she told him defensively, and so they were. She was missing the thick carpeting that had cushioned her journey downstairs, and it was a bit of a shock to be standing on ancient kitchen flagstones that seemed impervious to the central heating. Almost as much of a shock as Ivo saying her feet were beautiful.

'Here, put these on,' he said, kicking his moccasins off and bringing them over to her.

'No!' Tamsin exclaimed, instinctively shying away from any contact with him. 'I'm fine, honestly. I'll just sit down at the table. There's a carpet over there.'

'Put them on,' Ivo repeated, standing over her in a way that made her feel as fluttery as a captured butterfly. 'I'm just back from a Chinese winter, so everything here seems warm to me.'

It seemed easier to do as she was told, but as Tamsin did so she felt rebellious, too. It was a rebellion she decided cautiously to keep to herself for the time being, perhaps because Ivo's warmth was still in the soft material enclosing her feet, creating a certain intimacy that took her breath away.

If she wasn't careful, she chided herself, she might start thinking more silly things, like Ivo's surprising thoughtfulness making her feel cosseted as well as threatened. To take her mind off that, she stuttered nervously, 'Ch-China? You've been to Ch-China?'

'Yes, Ch-China,' he repeated, his teasing smile making her heart turn right over and come down wrong side up. Well, it must have done, or she wouldn't be so breathless, would she?

'You're mocking me,' she accused, but her sense of

humour was responding to his, calming her nerves, relaxing her.

'Perhaps I am, but sometimes you make it irresistible,' Ivo confessed, his big bare feet taking him back to the hob, where he poured steaming coffee into two mugs set out on a tray. 'One way or another, you're the most entertaining female I've met in years.'

Tamsin wrinkled her straight nose fastidiously at that. 'I can just about live with the entertaining part, but the female is a bit basic, isn't it? I'm a woman. Twenty-three years old and pushing twenty-four.'

Ivo carried the tray to the table and pulled out a chair invitingly. 'You don't look as though you're pushing very hard. To be on the safe side, though, come over here and sit before old age strikes you down where you stand.'

He was being absurd, but it was an absurdity that was very hard to resist. Tamsin couldn't help smiling as she flippered her way towards him, which was the only way she could keep her feet inside his outsize footwear. It was a relief to sit down and tuck her feet out of the way.

She was very conscious of his hands on the back of her chair, and she wished he wouldn't be quite so solicitous at making sure she was comfortably settled before he went to sit opposite her. She didn't want him to be courteous or charming, or anything at all that she admired in a man. She wanted him to carry on being horrid and hateful so that she could feel safe.

It was very important to her, at this stage in her life, to feel safe.

She was brooding on that and taking a cautious sip of the boiling coffee when Ivo asked bluntly, 'Why is my being a Gemini an important factor in our relationship?'

Tamsin choked, swallowed coffee that was much too hot, and spluttered, 'It isn't—and we don't have a relationship.'

Ivo's eyes strayed to the clock on the kitchen wall and returned thoughtfully to her face. 'We're in the witching hour, we're all alone, we've quarrelled, made up and damned nearly made love, and we're sharing coffee while a gale rages outside. If that doesn't make for a relationship, what does?'

Tamsin looked involuntarily towards the curtained windows. She'd all but forgotten about the gale, and becoming aware that it was still raging as fiercely as ever made her feel glad to be safe inside. It also made the kitchen seem cosy and intimate. If the intimacy also seemed to spread itself to her and Ivo, that was just an illusion, wasn't it?

She needed to think so, anyway, and so she replied, 'Any relationship you and I have is purely accidental. There's nothing personal in it.'

'Isn't there?' Ivo stretched out a hand and touched a wayward strand of fair hair at her temple, and it promptly curled around his finger. His expression changed, and for a split-second Tamsin thought that it was tenderness that softened the harsher planes of his face.

She sat quite still, mesmerised, until he took his hand away. She felt quite strange. His had been the lightest of gossamer touches, and yet every nerve in her body was still tingling responsively. And that fleeting expression. Had it really been there, or had she just imagined it?

What on earth was happening to her? Was it because

she was so very much alone with him that she was reacting so personally to everything he said and did? Yes, that must be it! If they were having coffee in her London home, with Gemma close by, she probably wouldn't be sensitive to him at all. Her reactions were only abnormal now because the circumstances were abnormal.

She felt a lot better once she'd figured that out, but Ivo said with the shrewdness she'd already come to expect from him, 'Our relationship must be personal if you have to think that long about it before you can answer me. And you know it.'

Tamsin gave a quick negative shake of her head. 'Stop putting words into my mouth.'

'I won't have the chance if you talk to me.' Ivo put his elbows on the table, leaned his chin on his linked fingers and studied her closely. 'Start by telling me if all house-sitters get their hair cut by top crimpers, have beautifully manicured nails and wear designer clothes.'

Tamsin drew in her breath with an audible gasp, thought about trying to bluff him, then sensed she wouldn't get away with it. 'Well done, Sherlock,' she quipped. 'If the game's up, I suppose I'd better confess that I'm not really a house-sitter at all.'

'I know damn well you're not,' he retorted. 'The gilt edge shows too much. So what are you?'

'I write romantic stories.'

His satirical eyebrows shot up. 'Successful, obviously, so why exactly are you masquerading as a sitter in this house?'

'Not from choice, I can assure you.' Tamsin hesitated, then said, 'It's a long story, so I won't bore you with the details. I'll be gone by tomorrow, anyway, when a regular sitter arrives to take over.'

'I don't care whether I'm bored or not, I want to know,' Ivo said stubbornly.

Tamsin's jaw jutted just as stubbornly as his, but as their eyes clashed she realised that he was perfectly capable of keeping her up all night until she told him all about it.

'All right,' she capitulated, 'I'll try to cram it in a nutshell. My sister Gemma runs a house-sitting agency. Your mother contacted her this morning wanting a sitter immediately because she had to make an unexpected journey to Cumberland.'

'Why?' Ivo demanded. 'That's where my sister Margaret lives.'

'Yes, she's gone to help your sister. From what I gather, Margaret's broken an arm, the twins and the home help are down with flu, the baby has croup, and her husband's away on an agricultural course.'

'Poor old Margaret,' Ivo sympathised. 'She's normally pretty shock-proof, so she must be in a state, but why didn't my mother call in old Sam Dewson from the village? He always looks after things when she's away.'

'Your mother was in such a tearing hurry that she didn't have time to explain much, but she did say her regular help was in hospital having a hernia operation. Anyway, normally my sister would have had no problem sending up a sitter right away, but your mother needed somebody experienced with horses and Gemma didn't have anybody who could cope with big animals available for another twenty-four hours.'

Tamsin shrugged, then continued wryly, 'It was at that point that I was misguided enough to return from Corfu after researching the background for the short story I'm working on now. I know horses, so, what with Gemma appealing to family loyalty and claiming that the reputation of her agency was at stake, I found myself straight back in my car and driving up here.'

She broke off, then concluded feelingly, 'I wouldn't mind so much, but Gemma swore it would be a doddle!'

'And then I blew in on the gale and scared you witless,' Ivo said with a smile.

Tamsin still felt touchy about that, so she protested, 'If I'd been scared witless I would have cowered in my room, not gone out to confront you, wouldn't I?'

'If you call fainting at my feet confronting me——'

'I didn't faint because of that!' Tamsin exclaimed.

'Then why?'

'Because. . .because. . .'

'Because I'm a Gemini?' Ivo suggested.

'No! I didn't know that then, did I?'

'True, but you soon made a point of finding out.'

'Only because——' Tamsin broke off as she realised how cunningly he'd led her on to the one subject she was determined not to discuss, and how completely she'd fallen into his trap.

She retreated into dignity, replying loftily, 'There's no point in explaining. You wouldn't understand.'

'Try me,' he suggested softly.

'No!'

'Coward,' he goaded her. 'Faint-hearted coward.'

'If you mention the word "faint" one more time, I'll brain you!' Tamsin exclaimed. 'I had no recollection of seeing your photograph in the sitting-room, but my subconscious must have somehow worked it into the short story I'm writing. I thought it was just a figment of my imagination, so you can imagine what a shock it was when I suddenly came face to face with you. Now do you understand?'

'I'm trying, but the Gemini bit is still blowing my

mind. It was important enough for you to mention, but not important enough for you to explain. That's a bit contradictory, isn't it?'

Ivo, Tamsin thought with exasperation, was like a bulldog. Once he latched on to something, he never let go. 'My interest in your star sign isn't personal, it's professional,' she explained reluctantly.

'You mean you're an astrologer on top of everything else?'

'No,' she responded, her exasperation deepening. 'A woman's magazine is planning a big horoscope supplement, and I've been commissioned to write a short romantic story especially for it. It has to be about a couple with compatible star signs.'

'The penny is beginning to drop,' Ivo encouraged her, 'but not far enough yet. Go on.'

'I'm an Aquarian, so I thought it would be easier to have an Aquarian heroine. I mean, I *know* myself. I did some research for a compatible hero and...' Tamsin broke off, floundering, her cheeks becoming uncomfortably warm.

An unholy gleam of amusement lighted Ivo's eyes. 'And you discovered that Gemini is a compatible hero for an Aquarian heroine,' he finished for her. 'You and I, in fact.'

'I can only repeat, there's nothing personal in it, and that my interest in you as a Gemini is purely professional,' she told him, not quite truthfully.

'So long as it's pure something, I'm game,' Ivo told her with a wicked smile. 'I don't mind offering myself up on the altar of the arts, so consider me a living bit of research material. I won't even ask you to be gentle with me. Where would you like to start? With a kiss, a caress, or straight into complete abandon?'

Ivo, Tamsin realised wrathfully, obviously regarded the whole thing as a joke. 'Very funny,' she told him pithily, 'but I happen to take my writing very seriously.'

'I take my love-life very seriously,' Ivo promptly countered, 'and you did say it was a romantic story.'

'Yes, definitely romantic, not a sexual fantasy, so let's drink our coffee and forget all about it, shall we?'

'Are you always such a spoil-sport?' he asked. When she pointedly refused to be goaded any further he went on, 'Anyway, your coffee's cold and mine's finished. I'll get some fresh.'

Tamsin watched him while he reheated the percolator, and discovered that there was something about his lithe, athletic build that her eyes liked to linger on, as though looking at him was a pleasure in itself.

Dismayed and embarrassed, she reminded herself frantically that Ivo was an unashamed womaniser, and that this was real life, *her* life. She mustn't let him intrude on it and wreck it the way he'd wrecked her story. She mustn't!

CHAPTER THREE

WHEN Ivo came back with fresh coffee he settled opposite Tamsin again, fixed her with a searching look and asked intently, 'These romantic stories that you write—do you base them on your own experiences?'

She shifted uncomfortably in her chair, not wanting to confess to him of all people that so far real life had never lived up to her dreams, so that she was forced to draw heavily on her imagination.

'Partly,' she prevaricated, and, seeing that a dissatisfied frown was lowering his eyebrows, she added, 'but I mix in other things, too.'

'What sort of things?'

He was showing that bulldog quality again of not giving up until he got what he wanted, Tamsin thought, shifting even more uncomfortably in her chair. 'Er—causes I'm interested in, and things like that,' she threw in wildly.

'What sort of causes?' he insisted.

'You wouldn't be interested,' she told him repressively.

'Run some past me and I'll let you know.'

Exasperated, Tamsin started, 'Endangered species——'

'That's me,' Ivo interrupted, his dark eyes gleaming with humour. 'I'm a bachelor. You can't get a species more endangered than that. If you and I shared an experience—say, a passionate experience—wouldn't that make an interesting story for you?'

'You're mixing me up with your ex-mistresses,' Tamsin told him drily. 'I write fiction, not smutty confessions for the tabloid scandal sheets.'

A flash of anger wiped the humour from Ivo's eyes, and he said with threatening softness, 'You use your claws in more ways than one, don't you, Tamsin?'

She felt a little thrill of danger, but she wouldn't back down. 'I wouldn't want any more misunderstandings to arise between us. You thought once that I was a tease. Now you can be certain that I'm not, and that I've no intention of becoming your next mistress.'

'I wasn't aware that I'd asked you to be,' he returned cuttingly.

Tamsin felt crushed, and fought the urge to storm off to her bedroom. That would be too much like a craven retreat, though, and her pride wouldn't let her give him the satisfaction of calling her a coward again.

To increase her discomfort, she was deeply aware of his brooding gaze. She resolutely refused to meet it, hoping that the leisurely way she was sipping her coffee made her look unconcerned.

'What time are you leaving tomorrow?'

Tamsin almost jumped at the abruptness of his question but answered it as calmly as she could, just in case it was his way of defusing the tension that was crackling between them. 'My replacement should be here by early afternoon. I'll be leaving right after that.'

She paused, then cautiously asked a question of her own. 'How about you—will you be staying on?'

Ivo shook his head. 'There's no point in visiting my mother if she's not here. I'll drive on up to Cumberland first thing in the morning.'

Another little chill touched Tamsin but she couldn't quite define what it was—not sadness, surely, that she would soon be parting from a man she'd never wanted to meet? No, it couldn't be! If she was aware of his physical attraction in a most uncomfortable way then the sooner they parted the better, particularly as he was a man who traded mercilessly on that sort of thing.

He loved lightly and never for long, while she loved cautiously and committedly. Hey, she checked herself with horror, what are you thinking about love for? There was no way love came into this, unless saying hello and goodbye to Ivo in the space of a few hours was all in the very best tradition of romantic fiction.

Naturally, as a writer she'd respond to that, and if she felt a bit peculiar in the region of her heart then that must just be a peculiar sort of relief.

Tamsin realised she'd been quiet much too long, brooding almost, and when she glanced at Ivo she was surprised to see that he looked as though he was brooding, too. 'How long will you stay in Cumberland?' she asked, just for something to say.

'Five, maybe six days. I've got some heavy work commitments and I'm only in England until the weekend after next. How about you?'

'I've got a Monday deadline on my astrological story. That normally wouldn't be a problem, but the story I'd planned isn't working out right. I think I'll have to scrap it and start again.'

'Because I intruded on it?' he asked.

'No,' she replied, almost blushing at the fib and realising with a sinking feeling that she'd have to add to it to make it sound convincing. 'I—er—think that maybe I haven't researched the astrological side thoroughly enough. I'm a bit—er—hazy in certain areas.'

Like why a Gemini and an Aquarian were supposed

to be kindred souls, she added to herself, when she and Ivo seemed more like chalk and cheese.

He was looking at her so thoughtfully that she suspected he knew she was being evasive, but for once he didn't press her to be more precise, and asked instead, 'Do you have any heavy personal commitments?'

'If you mean a boyfriend, no, and I mean to keep it that way. I want to concentrate on my career,' Tamsin replied, glad to be able to give an honest answer. 'In fact, the only thing I'm heavily committed to right now is personal freedom.' She thought for a moment, then added wryly, 'I imagine we have that much in common.'

Ivo hesitated momentarily, then agreed, 'We do.'

Was there regret in his voice, or was she only imagining it because she felt an inexplicable quiver of regret herself? Again, Tamsin felt uneasy. She didn't want to feel regret, or anything remotely like it. The big bonus of fighting herself free of her entanglement with Simeon had been that her life had become so simple, so clearcut. She desperately wanted to keep it that way.

A silence fell between them, but Ivo was still looking at her in that disconcertingly thoughtful way. Brightly, much too brightly, she switched the attention from herself to him, 'You said you'd just come back from China. What on earth were you doing there?'

'Photographing pandas. I'm doing a wildlife calendar of endangered species. Eagles in America, tigers in India, that sort of thing.'

Tamsin exclaimed in surprised disbelief, 'I thought you only photographed the rich and famous for impossibly lucrative fees!'

'I've noticed you're inclined to jump to conclusions,' he replied wryly, 'but I take a year off here and there to do something that offers a new challenge.'

THE THREAD OF LOVE

Tamsin was impressed by this new view of Ivo, so different from everything she'd ever read about him, but she was still sceptical enough to comment, 'Or to run away from a scandal that's become too hot for comfort?'

'Your claws are showing again,' he scowled. 'I'd have kept my mouth shut, except that I thought you were interested in endangered species.'

He had a point there, and Tamsin said contritely, 'Sorry, I didn't mean to be spiteful. I'd give my eye-teeth for an assignment like that. You've no idea how much I envy you.'

'I used to envy myself. Now I'm not so sure,' Ivo replied, so obscurely and curtly that Tamsin was baffled. She was rapidly becoming accustomed to his quicksilver personality, his lightning changes of mood, but in the blinking of an eye he seemed almost a different person.

Even the stubble on his chin seemed darker, pricklier, more aggressive. How very. . .manly. . .he was, though. And how very. . .female. . .he made her feel.

Tamsin couldn't stop herself wondering what it would be like to feel that rough stubble against her own smooth skin. As she wondered, an unwanted but inescapable thrill of excitement heated her blood, parted her lips and stained her cheeks with betraying colour.

Ivo stared at her, and his brown eyes darkened to almost black. He leaned across the table and touched her vulnerable lips with fingers that weren't quite steady, then breathed, 'Damn you, Tamsin.'

She had no idea why she was being cursed, but she thought he must be responding as reluctantly as she was to the same wild longing that had just shaken her to the core. This is madness, she told herself, and she tried frantically to calm the rapid racing of her heart.

But there was no such thing as calm while Ivo was touching her lips, making them tremble with desire. She wanted to kiss his fingers, nibble them, provoke him as he was provoking her. She wanted——Oh, it was insane, the things she wanted! Absolutely insane!

Suddenly Ivo frowned and pulled his fingers away from her lips as though her breath had scorched him. 'You know I want you, don't you?' he demanded.

Tamsin's racing heart almost stopped altogether, unused to such shocking bluntness. She thought of prevaricating, but all she'd learned of Ivo so far warned her that in his present mood he wouldn't settle for anything less than a straight answer.

'Yes, I know,' she admitted.

'And you want me.'

That was going much too far and much too fast for her, and she exclaimed, 'No!'

'Don't go coy on me, woman. Tell the truth for a change.'

Resentment flared through Tamsin. She felt she was being cornered, pushed into something she wasn't ready for. However intense her physical reaction to him might be, she'd no intention of being swept off her feet.

'I said, tell the truth for a change,' he repeated. 'I know damn well you want me.'

Stung, she retorted, 'If I do, it's something I can live with. I don't exist on a physical level the way you do. I'm not a one-night stand.'

'I know that, but I'm having trouble living with it,' he told her savagely. 'All my instincts tell me to seduce you, and I would if only you weren't so—so. . .'

Tamsin didn't want to be dragged into even deeper waters, and yet the way he suddenly broke off tantalised her beyond endurance. She waited for him to go on, and when he didn't she couldn't stop herself from asking, 'If only I weren't so—what?'

'Nice.'

Tamsin was flabbergasted, and asked involuntarily, 'What's wrong with being nice?'

'Nice girls are the easiest to love and the hardest to leave. It leads to pangs of conscience afterwards, and I don't like pangs of conscience.'

'My heart bleeds for you!' she exclaimed, incensed. 'Is there anything else you don't like?'

'I don't like being frustrated. Given the sort of girl you are, and the sort of man I am, have you got any bright ideas what we can do about it?'

'How about talking about something else?' she snapped.

Ivo stared at her, then his stormy look vanished and he burst out laughing. 'Only a nice girl could have said something as ridiculous as that,' he said.

His laughter, the warm look in his eyes, did funny, softening things to Tamsin, and because she didn't want to soften she bridled, 'So you think I'm funny, do you?'

'Funny, and getting more desirable by the minute. If you don't go in for one-night stands, what about two nights?' he suggested outrageously. 'That's not quite so basic, so it should ease that respectable conscience of yours.'

It wasn't Tamsin's conscience that was troubling her, but her distaste for Ivo's total lack of morals and her fear of getting trapped in any kind of involvement again. But all that was too heavy to explain to a man who was little more than a stranger, and so she sought for an answer he would find believable and acceptable.

'What,' she improvised 'if two nights led to three, and then to four or more? Before we know where we are, we could end up involved, cramping each other's lives, maybe even hating each other. I know I've made it plain that I don't *approve* of the sort of man you are, but I don't want to have a personal reason for hating you.'

Ivo flung himself back in his chair, stared at her broodingly for several moments, then admitted reluctantly, 'I don't want to hate you, either. How the hell did we get into this?'

'Because you wouldn't talk about something else!'

'I'm a man,' he growled. 'When I want a woman there *is* nothing else.'

Tamsin's pulses fluttered alarmingly, but she was piqued enough to point out, 'Then it's just as well I'm being sensible.'

'If you're as sensible as you think you are you'll go to bed,' Ivo responded with another surge of his volatile temper.

'But that's only evading the issue and——'

'Now!' he roared, standing up to tower over her.

'You're the most unreasonable man it's ever been my misfortune to meet!' Tamsin jumped to her feet and glared at him, too angry to let herself be intimidated. 'And there's no need to shout, I'll be glad to go. I should have known I couldn't have a reasonable conversation with you. When it comes to sex, you're the same as every other man—all you want is to grab first and hope there won't be any awkward questions afterwards!'

She began to stalk towards the door, but she'd forgotten she was wearing his outsize moccasins and she tripped out of them. She managed to right herself, but before she could stalk on, Ivo caught her arm and swung her round to face him.

He looked in the devil of a temper, so much so that

she began belatedly to feel intimidated. She tried to hide it by bluffing, 'What do you think you're doing?'

'I'm being the same as every other man,' he told her bitterly. 'I'm grabbing. . .'

His strong arms came around her, his head lowered menacingly and his lips closed forcefully over hers. Tamsin's senses reeled, outrage and desire becoming inextricably mixed as her body weakened under the force of his assault. She wanted to succumb, she wanted to resist, she wanted—oh, she didn't know what she wanted!

But the wild excitement pulsing through her veins was headier than any emotion she'd ever felt before she'd met Ivo, suspending rational judgement and igniting a passion so fierce that her body willingly moulded itself to his. And yet somehow, through it all, her senses still retained enough tattered shreds of civilisation to be appalled by her primitive reaction to him.

Ivo's lips might be thrilling her, but they were cheapening her, too. This desire rampaging through their locked bodies was just a parody of what might have existed between them if they'd got to know each other more slowly, more conventionally, and she wanted to cry because she knew it but he didn't.

Or did he? Was that why he suddenly thrust her away from him? Or was it because he still retained some tattered shreds of civilisation, too? Ivo didn't give her time to work it out. He was breathing harshly, and his voice was just as harsh as he ground out, 'If I ever tell you to go to bed again, do it right away—don't hang around to argue.'

Tamsin tried to tell him that she wouldn't, but the words never came. She was too confused, too stunned by the passion that had been unleashed so suddenly between them and then just as suddenly withdrawn.

She felt completely disorientated and could only stumble away from him on legs that had become too weak to support her. She staggered, but Ivo had turned his back on her, and somehow she managed to regain her balance, get out of the kitchen and up the stairs.

Once in her room, she changed rapidly into her pyjamas and collapsed into bed. She pulled the duvet up over her head as though it were some kind of protection against all the emotions that had shattered her during her short acquaintanceship with Ivo.

Acquaintanceship? What a ridiculous word to use! She'd damned nearly been seduced by the man, so, whatever he was to her, he was a great deal more than an acquaintance! Tamsin whimpered like a wounded animal as it gradually dawned on her that not everything in a relationship could be measured in hours, or days or weeks—not the way Ivo made her feel, not the way she was feeling still. . .

Oh, but had he had to sound so loving, so sincere, when he'd said she was funny and getting more desirable by the minute? He wasn't sincere at all and he didn't know anything about loving. He was a man who used women then discarded them. She was a woman who couldn't accept that sort of treatment.

Surreptitiously, under cover of the duvet, Tamsin touched her lips. They felt tender, as bruised as all her feelings. Next, her hand strayed wonderingly across her cheeks. They felt tender, too. At least she didn't have to wonder any longer what Ivo's rough stubble would feel like against her soft skin. She knew, and she wasn't likely to forget. Ever.

Nor, Tamsin realised with a pang that increased from

hurt to outright pain, was she ever likely to forget Ivo himself. Where was he now? Still downstairs, presumably, although he was the one who should really be in bed.

His day had been even more frantic than hers, flying into London, then motoring all the way up here to be met by a gale—and an unknown female brandishing a lethal-looking brass lamp.

In spite of herself, Tamsin smiled, and then she found herself reflecting that not once had he shown any sign of weariness. Quite the reverse! He must have enormous reserves of stamina...but then, of course, he was superbly fit, magnificently strong.

Tamsin's breath caught as she recalled exactly how fit and strong he was, and she swallowed hard and wished she had the sense to fall asleep herself. If only to give her a break from her racing thoughts and equally racing heart...

Fatally restless, though, she strained to identify some noise different enough from the raging elements outside to indicate where Ivo was. She desperately needed to know exactly where he was in relation to herself. Never mind what she'd just gone through, she still wanted him close. Not close enough to be threatening, of course, but close enough to be comforting.

Comforting? Ivo? Good heavens, Tamsin thought, her brain must be as shaken up as her body! In fact, if this were a story instead of real life, she'd give it up for lost—just as she had with her own story earlier. But, although she had a natural writer's ability to live her stories for the length of time it took her to write them, none had ever bruised her emotionally in the way that Ivo had...

She was feeling distinctly wistful when a cursory

knock on her door made the adrenalin start pumping through her veins again. The door opened and light streamed in from the passage. Ivo was a big black shadow in the middle of it, a shadow that got bigger as he came towards her.

Tamsin knew she should be shouting at him to get out of her room, but not for the life of her could she utter a word. The dreadful thing—the truly dreadful thing!—was that she wanted to see him again. She didn't want to go to sleep with them hating each other. If hate was what it had been. . .

'I think I've been unreasonable,' he said, speaking with difficulty, as though apologising came hard to him. He put a tray down on the table, and went on, 'I've brought a peace offering.'

'What is it, your head on a platter?' she asked, striving for lightness, although her pulse was leaping around like the lights on a fruit machine.

'I'm rather attached to my head. Would you settle for a cup of hot chocolate instead?' Ivo sounded amused now, and Tamsin began to relax. Besides. . .hot chocolate! Nothing could be less sinister, less rapacious than that.

'Where's your bedside lamp?' he asked.

'Wherever I dropped it,' Tamsin replied. 'I was going to crown you with it when I thought you were a burglar, remember?'

'I'll get it, in case you still want to.'

Tamsin wanted to say that it was all right, she wasn't afraid of him now, but Ivo was on his way out of the room. She was sitting up in bed when he came back, the duvet pulled up respectably to her shoulders.

Ivo plugged in the lamp, switched it on and looked at her. 'My God, the red pyjamas again, and here's me, trying to be on my best behaviour. Here drink your chocolate. I'm not very good with apologies.'

'I guessed, but none's necessary,' she said a little shyly as she took the mug from him. 'I'd much rather we forgot all about it, if that's all right with you.'

'Are you always so forgiving?' he asked, sitting down on her bed and smiling quizzically at her.

'No,' she admitted, 'but it's all been very unusual, hasn't it? You—me—meeting as we did in the middle of the night. Very emotional, one way or another.'

'You mean if we'd met in Piccadilly Circus during the day we wouldn't have been attracted to each other?'

Tamsin sipped her drink and hoped like mad that she sounded convincing as she replied, 'We probably wouldn't have even noticed each other.'

'I'd have noticed you.' The growl was back in Ivo's voice, and an excited shiver ran up and down Tamsin's spine as he added, 'I'd like to think you'd have noticed me, too.'

Of course I would have done, she wanted to say, but this was such tricky ground that she thought it wisest not to answer at all. When Ivo got tired of waiting for her to reply he added astutely, 'Is this another of the those times when you'd rather talk about something else?'

'Please,' she replied gratefully.

'All right, then. Tell me about yourself.'

'I already have,' she protested.

'Not much. I haven't a clue where you live.'

'In a big old house in Kensington with my sister Gemma. She runs her agency from the ground floor, we have a communal living area above that, then separate flats on the top two storeys. You live in Hampstead, don't you?'

'You do read the papers well,' he murmured. 'If you're a Londoner, where did you get to know about horses?'

'Oh, I've only been living in London for a couple of years. I was born and bred in the New Forest, where horses are a way of life. I've still got my own one, as a matter of fact, at my parents' place.'

'I like a country girl,' Ivo mused. 'Probably because I'm a country boy.'

A long time ago, Tamsin thought, wishing wistfully that she'd known him then. But she hadn't, and whatever Ivo might have been in the past, she'd be crazy to cherish any sentimental illusions about him now. She drank her chocolate in thoughtful silence, a silence Ivo did nothing to break.

When she'd finished he took her empty cup from her, put it on the bedside table, and ordered, 'Close your big beguiling eyes, and I'll take myself off to bed.'

Tamsin snuggled down and closed her eyes. She felt warm again, comforted, no longer bruised and upset as she waited for him to switch off the light and leave her. It had been nice of him to come here to make his peace with her. She liked him for that...

But why was he taking so long about leaving her? His weight was still depressing one side of her bed. Was he looking at her? If he was, it wouldn't be very wise to open her eyes to meet his. Downright foolhardy, in fact.

As the seconds passed, Tamsin couldn't bear the suspense that was building up within her. She opened her eyes a fraction to peer at him, then opened them wide. Ivo wasn't looking at her. He was reading something. She sat up indignantly, frowning to see what it was.

Heavens, it was her notebook! Blushing painfully, she

snatched it out of his hands. 'Don't read that! It's—it's—private. Where did you get it from?'

Ivo frowned at her vehemence, and replied, 'The waste-paper basket. I thought it had fallen from the table, so I was going to put it back, but I got interested. What's the panic all about? It doesn't read much like a state secret.'

'It doesn't read much like anything,' Tamsin retorted. 'It's the short story I was writing, the one that went wrong. I'm going to scrap it.' As proof, she tore the page out of the notebook, screwed it up and tossed it away.

'It read all right to me.' Ivo retrieved the page from the floor and smoothed it out again. 'Not my sort of thing, but——'

Tamsin tried to grab it from him. 'Of course it's not your sort of thing! It's written for women!'

He held it tantalisingly out of her reach and asked, 'What's this title about, *The Thread of Love*?'

She glared at him and explained awkwardly, 'According to my research, when a Gemini and an Aquarian have had a—well, say a passionate relationship, and they split up, there's still supposed to be a good deal of feeling left between them. A—a sort of thread of love, if you like, that still joins them.'

'Very poetic,' Ivo murmured, then before she could stop him he began to quote the opening lines of her story,

'David's feather-light kisses traced the line of her jaw and continued their sensuous journey of exploration downwards until he found the throbbing nerve where her neck joined her shoulder. Maria sighed and winced in the most delicious torment, and the pressure of his lips increased demandingly.'

'Stop it,' Tamsin demanded in an agony of embarrassment, not because she was ashamed of what she had written but because she didn't want Ivo ridiculing it. Anybody else, and she'd had given as good as she got, but she couldn't seem to overcome her peculiar sensitivity to him.

'You're being a spoil-sport again,' he teased. 'I'd no idea you wrote such torrid stuff. Why didn't the story work out? Are you sure it isn't because your subconscious substituted me for David?'

'Of course I'm sure,' Tamsin blustered. 'Some stories just go wrong sometimes, and that's all there is to it.'

'Perhaps we could put it right if I actually became David and you became Maria,' he suggested. 'It's worth a try, anyway. You did say you had a deadline on it, didn't you?'

'Yes, b-but——'

'Then let's get to it,' Ivo broke in, brushing aside her protests. 'Now, let's see...' He looked serious enough as he consulted the crumpled page, then quoted again, '"David's feather-light kisses..." Right, I've got that lot, right down to where "the pressure of his lips increased demandingly". Here we go, then. Relax, Tamsin, this experiment might just salvage your story.'

Before she could gather her scattered wits together sufficiently to object, Ivo began to plant light, lingering kisses along the line of her jaw.

'Ivo, stop it,' she gasped as each kiss struck sparks off the passion slumbering unwanted within her.

'Sssh,' he breathed against her skin. 'I haven't begun my sensuous journey of exploration downwards yet.'

THE THREAD OF LOVE

He began to kiss the sweet curve of her neck, and Tamsin's polished fingernails dug into the palms of her hands as she willed herself to feel nothing, nothing at all. But Ivo betrayed her by pulling aside the silk collar of her pyjama jacket and kissing the throbbing nerve where her neck joined her shoulder.

She winced in the most delicious torment, just like her heroine; and just like her hero, Ivo responded by increasing the pressure of his lips. Tamsin's head began to swim but she retained enough sense—just!—to gather up all her strength, moral and physical, to push him away from her.

'That wasn't in the plot,' he protested huskily.

'Consider it just written in,' she retorted, wishing she didn't sound quite as breathless as she did. 'I think you've taken the joke quite far enough.'

'Joke?' he asked. 'Who's joking?'

'You'd better be,' she told him grimly, 'otherwise this is the most infamous attempt at seduction I've ever come across, and I've come across a few.'

Ivo had the nerve to grin at her, a frankly boyish grin that tugged at her heartstrings, as, she suspected, it was meant to. 'I know exactly what you're going to say next,' she breathed between clenched teeth. 'You're going to say that I can't blame a fellow for trying it on. Well, I do! You came to me with hot chocolate as a peace offering, you said. I believed you and—and trusted you!'

Tamsin's voice almost broke with something that was more than indignation, so that she had to pause and swallow hard before she could continue, 'And all the time it was only a ruse so that you could have another shot at seducing me. That's—that's worse than infamous, Ivo. It's criminal!'

His grin vanished, and his dark eyebrows drew together ominously. 'You, Tamsin,' he accused in his turn, 'were giving me what I call more than the right degree of co-operation.'

'You were hoping I was, you mean,' she retorted bitterly.

'It was more than hope,' he continued inexorably. 'For a moment there we forgot all about David and Maria. We were ourselves, and it was working out fine. I could have sworn you got carried away, too. How come you didn't?'

If only he knew how very nearly she had, Tamsin thought with a shudder of fright, or was it shame? But he mustn't guess. The way she was still feeling about him, she didn't think she could summon up the strength to resist another onslaught.

'How come, Tamsin?' he repeated angrily, his words striking her like individual icy missiles.

She bit her lip and replied slowly, 'A woman has to fight harder for what she wants than a man does, Ivo. It's so much easier for her to be side-tracked—and I've no intention of being side-tracked. There are too many other things more important to me than that kind of thing. I thought I'd made that plain enough already.'

'How can you say that after the way we were a few moments ago?' he demanded.

'Because I know I'll feel differently tomorrow. I don't live just for the moment the way you do, and if you'd listened to *anything* I've said you'd have figured that out for yourself and not tried to pull a stunt like that.'

Ivo got to his feet and stood looking down at her enigmatically. Then he challenged, 'It might have started out as a stunt, but that wasn't the way it finished up. Or are you incapable of ever being completely honest?'

Tamsin's heart lurched in the most uncomfortable fashion. She didn't want to lie to him, she really didn't, but she didn't see what else she could do. 'As far as I'm concerned, it was always a stunt, a stunt that didn't pay off,' she insisted.

'Then I'll quit wasting your time—and mine. Goodnight, Tamsin.' His politeness was cold, cold as charity, and just as humiliating.

'Goodnight,' she echoed hollowly.

The light snapped off. The door opened and closed and Ivo was gone. Tamsin knew that this time he wouldn't be coming back. Somehow, that knowledge gave her no comfort at all.

CHAPTER FOUR

TAMSIN knew from experience that she wasn't going to sleep. She never could when she was over-tired or had something on her mind, and tonight—thanks to the devil who was Ivo Durand!—she was both.

She lay listening to the gale as the minutes passed, fuming that she'd allowed herself to be deceived by what she'd taken as a genuine gesture of reconciliation, of friendship.

She should have known better, she berated herself. Ivo's behaviour was typical of his light attitude to love, and with his lack of conscience he'd probably fallen asleep the moment his head had hit the pillow.

She could imagine him in his lordly arrogance dismissing her as a rather silly female who didn't know what she really wanted, and therefore not worthy of another thought. And that hurt much more than it should have done.

Tamsin was turning restlessly for the umpteenth time when suddenly there was a crashing on the roof above her head, and then another, followed by the sound of breaking glass.

Almost before she realised it she was out of bed, running out of the room and flicking on light switches as she raced downstairs in the direction of the noise. Good grief, on top of everything else that had happened to her tonight, all she needed was the house to fall down about her ears. . .

As more glass smashed, Tamsin realised the noise

THE THREAD OF LOVE 61

was coming from the back of the house on her side, the guest wing. If Ivo was asleep he probably wouldn't even hear it. She ran into the big, formal dining-room that Mrs Durand had told her was hardly used these days, and more glass smashing drew her over to the windows.

She grasped the heavy velvet curtains to pull them back when a strong arm circled her waist, lifted her bodily and carried her back into the centre of the room. Ivo's voice, rough with anger, grated in her ear as he demanded, 'What the hell do you think you're doing?'

She was surprised to find he had been disturbed, but that was nothing compared with the shock of finding her soft silk-clad body once again clamped hard against the lean, hard strength of his.

For a moment so many bewildering sensations exploded through her that she couldn't answer, then finally she gasped, 'The gale! It's—it's breaking up the house. I must try to stop the damage.'

'By getting a faceful of flying glass? That's going to be a lot of help,' Ivo shouted, dropping her unceremoniously on to her feet and then swinging her round to face him.

'But—but I'm responsible,' she faltered, looking up into his dark, saturnine face. 'The whole idea of my being here is to make sure nothing happens to the house while your mother is away.'

'To the extent of taking on a gale bare-handed and——' his eyes flicked mockingly up and down the length of her quivering body '—barefoot?'

'I don't have time to think about things like that. I must do something!' she fretted.

'There's not a damn thing you can do except go back to bed.'

'But I'm *responsible*,' she repeated, stressing the word in another determined attempt to make him understand.

'And I, heaven help me, am responsible for you,' Ivo told her with a kind of enraged fatalism.

'You're not!'

'Of course I am. I'm a man and you're nothing but a muddle-headed, feather-brained female.'

'How *dare* you?'

'Oh, I dare,' Ivo mocked. 'Don't you know there's a conservatory out there?'

'Yes, but——'

'Then you should have enough sense to realise that if you pull those curtains back you could be cut to pieces by flying glass. Tiles from the roof are smashing down into the conservatory, and there's no guarantee that the dining-room windows aren't being damaged as well. Those curtains are protecting this room—and us. Can't you get that through your thick head?'

'There's no need to be insulting,' Tamsin flared, too angry at his contempt to see reason. 'I was going to rescue your mother's plants. She's got some rare species out there. She left almost as many instructions for their care as she did for the horses!'

Her indignation drained away as a fresh spectre raised itself and creased her forehead with anxiety. She darted round him, exclaiming, 'I'd better check the stables! Anything could be happening out there. Ouch!'

Her yell of pain came as Ivo grabbed her long fair hair and pulled her up short. 'You're not taking one step outside this house,' he told her forcefully. 'Anything could be *flying* around out there—tiles, branches, fences, you name it—and if you think you could keep to your feet then you don't know much about gales like this one.'

'But——'

'If I hear one more "but" out of you, so help me I'll wring your neck,' Ivo threatened, coiling her hair around his hand in a way that held her helpless and made her wince. 'The stables have walls two feet thick. They were built three hundred years ago and they'll still be standing in three hundred years time. The same goes for the barn, so don't start fussing about the cats, either. As for the plants, they'll have to take their chances, and that's precisely what my mother would say if she were here now.'

Tamsin was silenced, but she simmered with resentment. All right, so now that the situation was fully explained to her, everything that Ivo said made sense. That still didn't excuse the way he'd manhandled her, or the names he'd called her.

'You're hurting me,' she said coldly.

Ivo eased his grip on her hair, but only slightly. 'Hurting you?' he questioned sarcastically. 'The way I'm feeling right now, you're lucky I haven't murdered you. Life with you around is one riot after another. With the crazy things you do, it's a mystery to me how you've survived this long. Some man should have licked you into shape years ago.'

Tamsin's resentment heated to boiling point and spilled over. 'That's just the sort of comment I'd expect from an arrogant, overbearing, self-satisfied beast of a man like you,' she raged. 'You stand there looking civilised enough, but the truth is you're still trailing creepers from some primeval jungle. And just because I'm not as big and strong as you are, and just because I may be a bit impulsive sometimes, doesn't give you the right to——'

'Nobody has to give me rights, I take them,' Ivo

broke in, icily unimpressed and using his grip on her hair to steer her mercilessly towards the door, 'particularly when I have to deal with a female who can't tell the difference between impulsiveness and insanity.'

Tamsin, wincing but too proud to show her pain, had no choice but to walk with him, although she demanded, 'Where are you taking me?'

'To bed.'

'You wouldn't dare!'

'Don't tempt me,' Ivo responded laconically. 'I may be a primeval beast but I've no longer any intention of beating my chest and claiming territorial rights over you. This night has gone on so long that your ability to arouse me has dropped below your ability to infuriate me. Right now I'd swop you—and a dozen females like you—for a few hours' solid sleep. That, of course, is a situation that could change instantly if you don't behave yourself and shut up.'

Tamsin instinctively opened her mouth to protest, but Ivo was glowering at her and the challenging look in his dark eyes made her think better of it. Her proud spirit might be wounded by his insensitive, rough and ready ways, but that was nothing new when it came to him! Reaching the safety of her own room was what mattered most, after all.

Ivo, though, turned left at the top of the stairs into the family wing. He was still steering her by her hair, but she tried to turn back. 'Ouch!' she squealed again as the roots of her hair were pulled. 'My room's the other way.'

'Heaven only knows what you'll be up to next if I let you out of my sight. You, my girl, are going to sleep where I can keep tabs on you, and I warn you that I'm a very light sleeper.'

Aghast, Tamsin found herself pulled into his room, and her nerves jumped as Ivo slammed the door shut behind them. He steered her over to the far side of the bed, pulled back the covers, then lifted her up and tossed her in as unceremoniously as if she'd been a sack of coal. Then he threw the covers over her just as unceremoniously.

'I don't care if the whole damn roof blows away. There you stay until morning. OK?' he thundered.

Tamsin stared up at him with eyes like saucers, but there was no softening of his harsh expression. Then she noticed how drawn with fatigue his face was, and how dark were the shadows under his eyes. Big and powerful as he was, it was obvious that even Ivo had his limit, and he'd reached it. He was just about out on his feet.

'OK,' she whispered, succumbing to a pang of compassion she knew she must be out of her mind to be feeling. But feel it she did, and it was just one more in a whole bundle of things she was unable to do anything about right then.

Ivo growled something that was fortunately indecipherable, and walked away. The light flicked off, and moments later the other side of the bed depressed as he climbed in beside her. Tamsin slithered as far away from him as she possibly could without falling out on to the floor. Then she lay rigid, eyes wide open, brain frantically trying to interpret every move he made.

He only made one, and that was to turn his back on her as though she weren't there at all. Almost instantly his breathing became deep and regular. As she listened to it she realised that he was asleep. Slowly her own breathing relaxed and she felt fatigue overcoming her as the adrenalin that had kept her alert for so long stopped pumping through her veins.

Tamsin turned her head instinctively in the direction of the guest wing as the gale tore another tile from the roof and sent it crashing into the conservatory below, but the sounds were distant, muted, not half as frightening as when they'd been happening over her head.

With rapidly encroaching sleep sapping her willpower and softening her resentment, she began to view the man asleep beside her in a different light.

Much as she hated to admit she was wrong about anything, she conceded that Ivo wasn't always beastly. He'd been right to pull her back from those windows. Admitting that, even to herself, was a major concession for her to make and it led to another—that she felt truly safe for the first time in this traumatic night with his comforting bulk fast asleep beside her.

She tried to tell herself that Ivo and safety were opposing factors, but her brain was becoming hazy and her eyelids were too heavy to keep open any longer. Moments later her breathing softened and she stirred no more.

And, as she slept, Ivo gave up his pretence that he, too, was asleep. His eyes opened and he stared moodily into the night.

When Tamsin awoke the next morning she lay with her back to Ivo's side of the bed, but she sensed that she was alone.

Cautiously she turned over and, sure enough, Ivo had gone. Her hand strayed over to his side of the bed and up to his pillow, tracing the indent his dark head had made. Like the space he'd filled beside her, it was quite cold. He'd got up some time ago, then, and carefully enough not to disturb her. She wanted to think it was out of thoughtfulness, but suspected it might have been uninterest.

She didn't know how she would have dealt with waking up with him beside her, but, now that he'd spared her from that particular confrontation, she didn't exactly feel relieved. Almost disappointed, in fact.

Blast! That meant her feelings towards him were as ambiguous as ever—fiery attraction iced with extreme caution! She'd hoped so much, too, that she would awake to find the events of the night remote, perhaps even laughable—but never had she felt less like laughing.

In fact, she felt downright miserable, but that was hardly surprising, since the traumas of the night had survived to shadow a bright new day like a regretted hangover.

And, judging by the sunshine streaming into her room, it was a very bright day indeed. True, a stiff breeze was still disturbing the old window-frames, but not in a way that could be compared with last night's gale.

All of Tamsin's lingering sleepiness vanished as she thought about the gale and all that had happened during it. Given the mood Ivo had been in when he'd dumped her in his bed, she was pretty certain he'd be more determined than ever to make an early start up to Cumberland this morning, if only to be done with her. He might even have gone by now.

It would be shrewd to stay out of his way until she was sure, of course, but she couldn't. She had the animals to care for, then the gale damage to check, and she had no idea what time it was. Her wrist-watch with its alarm set for seven was in her own room, and here she was, still in Ivo's bed.

She was strangely reluctant to leave it, and she couldn't understand why she should want to prolong any contact, however remote, with a man who had bruised her as emotionally—and physically!—as Ivo had.

She didn't even feel quite the same girl as she'd been yesterday. Not totally shattered, perhaps, but—different. It must be something to do with the excitement that was beginning to ravage her nervous system at the prospect of seeing him again.

Did she never learn? Apparently not, Tamsin decided, realising that it was impossible to be excited and miserable at the same time, and that the excitement was definitely winning.

Muttering darkly to herself about being a glutton for punishment, she eased herself out of Ivo's bed as cautiously as if he were still in it—so powerful was his presence, even though he'd long since gone!—then hurried to her room.

She washed and dressed quickly in jeans and the heavy sweater that had failed to offer her any real protection when she'd gone downstairs to have coffee with him last night. In a moment of weakness she even found herself stroking the sweater in a dreamy, sentimental way, just because it had been crushed into Ivo's arms with her inside it.

Stop it! she scolded herself. You can't get sentimental about a man who would have seduced you and then swanned off to the next adventure without so much as a backward glance!

But, although her head was full of good advice, her heart wouldn't listen, and the excitement bubbling within her forced her to admit she'd be very sorry if Ivo had already gone. Just one last look at him, that was all she wanted, she promised herself. Just to prove that she was right about everything being different between them today.

Different and normal. After all, nothing could have been more abnormal than last night...strangers meeting at midnight in an isolated house while a frightening gale raged outside. In that sort of dynamic atmosphere, it would have been odd indeed if a predatory male and a young female hadn't felt some sort of attraction for each other.

Sighing for she knew not what, she brushed her hair, tied it up in a pony-tail, and began to panic as she realised she would feel dreadfully cheated if she didn't see Ivo again. The feeling was so strong that she didn't stop to analyse it, but hurried out of her room and ran down the stairs.

She nearly fell over his luggage in the lower passage, but she didn't mind. Those battered, much-travelled suitcases were proof that he was still here...

Tamsin hurried into the kitchen, suppressed excitement bringing a special glow to her scrubbed cheeks and adding a sparkling brilliance to her blue eyes. Then she caught her breath, because there was Ivo and, freshly shaved, he looked every bit as dishy as the prickly, passionate man who had beguiled and bedevilled her last night.

Restraint overcame her as she thought of the bed they'd shared, and, although nothing had happened, the intimacy of it lingered, at least for her. She felt too shy to study him as openly as she wanted to, but she risked letting her eyes rest on him a moment or two longer.

He was dressed pretty much as she was, in sweater and jeans, his dark wavy hair no longer dishevelled and flopping over his forehead but brushed neatly back.

What was more, he was sitting at the table drinking tea, and looking reasonably tame. Then he looked up, saw her and growled, 'Damn!'

Just one little word, but it hurt Tamsin immeasurably. She didn't know quite what she'd been hoping for, but not that, certainly not that. A little of her glow left her, and to cover up her dismay she said ironically, 'Good morning to you, too! Don't worry, I won't spoil your tea by joining you. I'll catch up on some later. I have the livestock to see to.'

With a great show of unconcern she walked past him towards the pantry to get the cats' food, but he caught her arm and sort of flicked her back so that the next thing she knew she was sitting down at the table with him.

'The animals can wait a few minutes,' he said, letting go of her arm and sitting back to survey her through narrowed eyes.

'I don't like to stay where I'm not welcome,' she retorted, meaning to be flippant, but somehow her hurt showed through.

'Every bit as awkward as I remember,' Ivo said reflectively, 'and just as desirable. That's why I was damning you. I was hoping that overnight you'd turn from a delectable princess into a frog or something. You just never co-operate, do you?'

Tamsin was bewildered. When she could, she said, 'Only princes turn into frogs, as far as I can remember, but this isn't a fairy-tale, Ivo.'

'It might as well be,' he replied cryptically, reaching for the teapot and pouring a cup of tea for her.

Tamsin wrinkled her nose, and confessed, 'I'm afraid I'm not with you.'

'Oh, yes, you are. Very much so. In fact, you're stuck

with me. *That's* why I was hoping you'd come hopping down as a frog so that, in weaker moments, I wouldn't fancy you any more.'

Tamsin looked at the teapot suspiciously. 'Is there something funny in the tea? If so, I'll settle for coffee. It wouldn't do for both of us to be raving.'

Ivo smiled, but none too pleasantly. 'If you think I'm raving, it's nothing to what you're going to be when you hear what's happened.'

Tamsin began to be seriously alarmed. 'You must have been drinking,' she accused, 'and at this time in the morning, too! Ivo, how could you?'

'I haven't touched anything stronger than tea, but I've got the brandy on stand-by for you,' he told her mockingly.

'Will you be sensible?' Tamsin exclaimed, exasperation rapidly overcoming her alarm.

Ivo glowered at her, leaving her in no doubt that the hostility she'd aroused in him last night was still his principal emotion towards her. 'I'm worn out from being sensible last night,' he told her savagely, 'and if you think I'm enjoying the situation, you're way out. We're marooned.'

'Marooned,' she echoed disbelievingly. 'We can't possibly be marooned! We're not on an island!'

'Yes, we are.'

'You sure it's not an ark, and at any moment the animals will come trooping in two by two?' she scoffed.

Ivo stood up and got hold of her pony-tail. He eased rather than yanked her to her feet, but Tamsin was in no mood to appreciate the difference. 'Ouch!' she protested. 'Let go, Ivo! My scalp's still sore from last night. Do you always have to be so—so darn physical?'

'Something about you never fails to arouse the beast

in me. I think it's the way you always assume that you're right and I'm wrong,' he replied grimly, marching her over to the kitchen window and letting go of her. 'Look out there.'

Tamsin flung him a sour glance, rubbed her suffering scalp, and looked out of the window. She looked a long time, her mouth falling open.

Ivo closed her mouth with a mocking finger. 'Now be a good girl and say you're sorry.'

She stared up at him, all eyes and disbelief, then turned her wondering gaze back to the window. When she'd arrived yesterday afternoon she'd admired the river winding its tranquil way through the rich pastures at the bottom of the shallow valley. But where the river had been there was now a wide swath of water. Not tranquil water like a lake, but a turbulent, seething torrent rushing seawards as though somebody had pulled the plug out of a gigantic drain.

'It can't be all around the house,' she gasped.

'It is. The village is on one hill, and we're on another—marooned, just as I said.'

'But—but how did it happen?' Tamsin stammered, unable to take in the enormity of what had happened.

'The river's burst its banks. It happened once before when I was a boy and a gale followed weeks of heavy rain. Those lower pastures were marshes before they were drained. I guess you could call it a case of the river reclaiming its own.'

'The bridge——'

'That's submerged as well. When I crossed it last night the river was pretty high; that's nothing unusual at this time of year, and I thought it would be down again this morning, but——' Ivo paused and grimaced '——I was wrong.'

'What about the road that leads north?'

'Unfortunately the same bridge connects us both ways. We're stuck here until the water goes down.'

Tamsin stared at him, still not quite able to take in what he was telling her. 'How long will that be?'

'I've no idea. When I was a boy we were cut off for three days.'

Three days! She and Ivo marooned together for three days! That was a lot different from a few hours. Anything could happen in three days...

'A boat,' she said desperately. 'I have to stay here until this afternoon to look after the animals, but couldn't you get off by boat?'

'I drove up the motorway, I didn't sail up.'

His sarcasm stung Tamsin and goaded her into retorting, 'Where there are rivers there are always boats! Couldn't somebody row across and get you?'

'That isn't a mill-pond out there, it's a flood, and it will be full of hazards like submerged trees, floating logs and goodness knows what else. People can't be expected to risk their lives except to try to save the lives of others. You and I might be inconvenienced, Tamsin, but we're not at risk.'

'No, of course not,' she admitted shamefacedly. 'I suppose helicopters are used to rescue people who are really in trouble?'

'Yes, but, since I've no intention of raping you, I don't think there are grounds for calling out one of those, do you?'

'There's no need to be offensive,' she retorted huffily. 'I'm sure you can be trusted—if you give me your word that you can.'

Ivo's face twisted bitterly and he turned away from her, going back to the table. 'You shouldn't need my word. You slept beside me last night and I didn't touch you.'

Tamsin trailed after him, sat down and picked up her cup of tea. As she sipped it she felt obliged to point out, 'You were exhausted.'

For a moment he didn't answer, then he said, 'I wasn't when I woke up this morning.'

Tamsin went pink at the thought of his waking up while she slept on. What if she'd woken up then? She still couldn't begin to guess how she'd have felt, but the possibilities made her knees feel weak, and she wasn't at all sure it was from panic.

'You're blushing,' Ivo said. 'I suppose that means you'd rather talk about something else.'

In spite of herself, Tamsin smiled. 'You're getting to know me pretty well.'

'Not half as well as I'm going to get to know you over the next few days.'

He sounded so morose that Tamsin was conscience-stricken. In her dismay she'd behaved as though their being stranded together were all his fault. Nothing could have been more unfair, particularly as he had every reason to resent their situation as much as she did.

'Ivo. . .?' she began tentatively.

'Yes?' He sounded more resigned than anything now.

Encouraged, Tamsin went on, 'How are we going to manage?'

He looked down at her anxious face and his own expression softened. 'Easy, no sweat,' he promised.

'Oh.' She wasn't altogether convinced, but she finished her tea, and sighed, 'At least we won't starve. There's not a lot in the freezer because your mother was called away too suddenly to stock up first, but there's enough food in the fridge and pantry to keep us going.'

'Unfortunately the fridge is de-frosting fast and the freezer will have to be emptied soon,' Ivo said. 'The power lines are down. Anything that will spoil will have to be cooked today.'

Tamsin gazed at him in wonder. 'Now you tell me! Well, tell me something else—how are we going to cook if there's no electricity?'

'The same way as I made the tea,' Ivo replied, nodding towards an ancient blackleaded stove built into one wall of the kitchen.

'That museum piece!' she gasped, swinging round to stare at it and noticing for the first time that the fire beside the oven had been lit. 'Does it actually work?'

'Sure it does. My mother still uses it for baking bread and the Sunday roasts in winter.'

'I'm not your mother!' she exclaimed in dismay.

'Do you think I haven't noticed?'

He sounded so surly—as if he were blaming her for the flood now!—that Tamsin decided they'd best stay apart while they each came to terms with the catastrophe. She got to her feet and said resolutely, 'If I'm going to spend the rest of the day battling with that antiquated oven the sooner I get the animals done, the better.'

She went into the pantry and put some cans of cat food, a carton of long-life milk, some plastic feeding bowls and a tin-opener into a basket, and when she came out Ivo was standing by the back door. She was surprised, and doubly so when he took the basket from her and followed her into the porch, where outdoor clothes hung from a rack, with wellingtons neatly paired on the floor underneath them.

'You're not in this on your own, you know,' he told her. 'I'll help.'

He was obviously making a real effort to get over his surly mood and, as always when he was being reasonable, Tamsin warmed towards him. Besides, she was beginning to feel she could do with all the help she could get, although she felt duty-bound to deny it.

'No, there's no need for that,' she told him. 'I'm here to hold the fort, remember. It's a case of you Robinson Crusoe, me Man Friday.'

'*Girl* Friday,' he corrected her, a glimmer of a smile easing his harsh expression. 'If you were a man I wouldn't be wondering how I'm going to keep my hands off you while we're penned up together for a few days.'

Tamsin wished he wouldn't keep referring to the sexual attraction between them. It didn't help matters at all. Nor did she see how his helping her would ease the situation, since it would only increase the time they spent together, and she opened her mouth to say so. Then it occurred to her that it wouldn't be good for a man as physical as Ivo to be kept idle, so she held her peace.

'Wise girl,' Ivo approved, definitely smiling now as he accurately interpreted the variety of emotions flitting across her face.

'Last night you didn't approve of me being wise,' she murmured, and could have kicked herself for mentioning something that was best forgotten.

Ivo obviously thought so, too, because he said, 'Given the circumstances we find ourselves in today, I think it's better if we stop thinking about last night—unless it gives you a perverse sort of pleasure.'

Tamsin blushed, then thought ruefully that during the past few hours she'd blushed more than she had in the past few years. When was she going to stop being so extraordinarily sensitive to him?

Ivo watched the blush creeping up her cheeks, put down the basket and rested his powerful hands on her shoulders. 'You think I'm a monster, don't you? Will it help if I tell you that I don't mean to be?'

'Not a lot,' she admitted frankly, wishing her heart wouldn't hammer so painfully when he touched her. 'What you say and what you do don't always bear much relation to each other. It's the Gemini factor.'

'What's that supposed to mean?'

Tamsin dredged up all the research she'd done for her short story, and explained, 'Twins are your birth sign—you're two people sharing one skin. You just can't help being contradictory. One minute you're charming, and the next you're. . .' She broke off, not wanting to cause another confrontation, not here in a porch that seemed to be getting smaller by the minute, especially with Ivo's hands still on her shoulders.

'I suppose that you, as an Aquarian, are an angel?'

'No, far from it,' Tamsin replied, reacting huffily to the sarcasm in his voice. 'I can be contradictory, too, but I'm certainly not obsessed with sex for its own sake!'

'And here endeth today's sermon,' Ivo mocked, a teasing smile lifting his firm lips as he imitated the intonation of a priest.

Tamsin wasn't amused. 'You shouldn't ask questions if you can't take the answers.'

Ivo gave her shoulders a none too gentle shake. 'Stop taking everything so seriously. You and I have got to learn to laugh together, otherwise the next few days are going to be hell.'

Tamsin caught her breath. He was right, of course. She'd never be making such heavy weather of everything if she'd been marooned with anybody but Ivo, but she didn't think it would be a good thing to tell him that. . .

CHAPTER FIVE

TAMSIN was very conscious of Ivo's hands on her shoulders, very conscious of his closeness altogether, and she felt a little awkward as she confessed, 'I don't usually take myself so seriously. I think there's something about you that brings out the worst in me.'

'That seems to be a mutual problem, so we'll both have to try harder to coexist more peacefully,' he said with a wry smile.

'Yes,' she agreed softly, smiling back.

Ivo released her, looked at the clothes rack and asked, 'Which coat is yours?'

'That one,' she replied, pointing.

Ivo unhooked the weatherproof jacket and held it out for her to slip her arms into. As she did so he said, 'A Barbour jacket, no less, and so well worn that it has to belong to a real country girl and not a yuppie pseud. It even smells of horses, as it should.'

'I don't know whether that's a compliment or an insult,' Tamsin replied, half laughing.

'From me, it's a compliment. I like the smell of horses. Mine smells the same, anyway,' he added, lifting down his own Barbour, which was even more decrepit than her own.

A far-away expression darkened his brown eyes, and his voice deepened as he went on, 'When I'm stuck in a city for longer than I like I think of this old jacket hanging here waiting for me, and I always feel better. It represents home for me as much as anything else around here, maybe even more.'

Tamsin's heart stood still. This, she thought wonderingly, was the real Ivo talking, as though he was at peace with himself for once. For all his considerable strength, he suddenly seemed vulnerable, and it affected her immeasurably.

This, she thought breathlessly, is a man I could love. If he could put his past behind him...if I could risk involving myself again . . . if——

But there was no time for any more ifs because Ivo had fallen silent, much too silent. Tamsin felt strangely cheated, and to prompt him into revealing more of his real self she said, 'I saw your jacket last night when I was hanging up my own after bedding down the horses. I wondered whom it belonged to. You don't have a father, do you?'

'No, like all good monsters, I was put together in a laboratory. Didn't you see the bolt through my neck when you caught me with my shirt off?' Ivo joked, and Tamsin sensed she'd said the wrong thing. She was sure of it when he continued, 'If you're fishing for information, my father isn't dead. He skipped off with another woman when I was twelve, and I haven't seen him since.'

Tamsin felt dreadful. 'I'm sorry,' she apologised. 'Sometimes I've got a big mouth.'

'It looks just about the right size to me, and very kissable with it,' Ivo responded, refusing to be serious again.

What, Tamsin thought in exasperation, was she supposed to do with such a man? He changed tack more often than a yacht in a cross-wind. Meanwhile, they were still pressed up far too close to each other. She kicked off her slippers, looked around for her boots, and swayed against Ivo as she thrust her feet into them.

'Sorry,' she said again, feeling all hot and bothered as his strong arms supported her.

'I never realised what a cosy place this porch is,' Ivo replied. 'If we get bored over the next few days we can always come out here to liven things up.'

'If that's your idea of peaceful coexistence I'll move into the barn,' Tamsin replied, trying to match his flippancy as she extricated herself carefully from his arms.

'You'd soon move back again. The cats are wild, you know,' Ivo replied, putting his own boots on. 'Strays, every last one of them.'

'Yes, I know. Your mother told me on no account to touch them. I wish she'd told you the same thing about me.'

'I'm sure she would have done if she'd known I was coming home.'

'Would you have listened?' Tamsin asked sceptically.

'Would you have wanted me to?'

The trouble with Ivo, Tamsin thought—at least, *one* of the troubles with Ivo!—was that there was no beating him with words. He could juggle them any way he liked to take advantage, and then control, of any given situation.

Temporarily giving up on him, she eased herself around his big frame and groped for the door-handle. When she found and turned it, she escaped into the cobbled stable-yard, gasping as the stiff breeze that was the legacy of the gale buffeted her jacket and whipped long strands of fair hair from her pony-tail.

She battled on, convinced that if she stopped walking she'd be blown right back to the house. She'd almost reached the barn when she realised she didn't have the basket of cat food. What with one thing or another, she'd forgotten all about it.

She turned back abruptly and bumped into Ivo, striding behind her with the basket. 'We'll have to stop meeting like this,' he said solemnly. 'People will begin to talk.'

Oh, he was impossible to resist, absolutely impossible! A bubble of laughter rose within her and escaped in a rich chuckle.

'That's better,' Ivo approved. 'I get heavy withdrawal symptoms when I don't hear you laugh often enough. What's more, I'm beginning to think you get heavy withdrawal symptoms when you don't bump into me often enough.'

'I do seem to be making a habit of it,' Tamsin admitted ruefully, 'but I forgot the basket.'

'I didn't.'

'So I see. Perhaps, as Robinson Crusoe, you have your uses.'

'As Girl Friday, you definitely have yours.'

Tamsin pulled a face at him but it was dawning on her that, since Ivo rarely took anything seriously, least of all her, the best thing she could do was to stop taking him seriously, as well.

After all, she was only encouraging him by getting hot and bothered every time he provoked her. If she stopped reacting so positively and played him back at his own game, perhaps he'd get discouraged and stop baiting her. It was worth a try, anyway.

'Why are you so quiet?' Ivo asked suspiciously as they walked on together to the barn.

'I was wondering if the cats would get indigestion if I threw you to them for breakfast,' she retorted, and he repaid her cheekiness by ruffling her already wind-ruffled hair.

They smiled at each other, and Tamsin's heart lurched a little because really friendly smiles weren't exactly common between them. Perhaps they were actually learning to coexist peacefully after all. There was certainly a special glow within her as she waited for Ivo to open the door of the barn.

It was, as he'd pointed out to her last night, an ancient barn, built to survive the worst the elements could hurl at it. Made of flint and brick, with a tiled roof that was steep enough to have once been covered by thatch, the newest thing about it was the iron-studded door, and that looked well over a hundred years old.

Tamsin asked as Ivo pushed the door open, 'How do the cats get in and out?'

'Through a ventilation window at the side. There's an old horse trough underneath it. The cats jump on that, up and through the window and land on the bales of straw on the other side. It's something the first stray who moved in here figured out, and the rest followed suit.'

'Real copy-cats, in fact,' she quipped as she walked forward to collect up the empty bowls she'd set out yesterday. Then she called, 'Hey, kitty-kitty. Hey, kitty-kitty.'

She counted the cats appearing from all over the barn and said to Ivo, 'I make it only nine. There were fourteen last night.'

'The number's rarely the same two days running,' he replied, getting busy with the tin-opener and the tins of food. 'Some of the cats come and go on a regular basis. Either they're persistent wanderers or they have another safe refuge somewhere, but the number doesn't normally drop this sharply. Some must have got cut off in the village by the flood.'

'What will happen to them?' Tamsin asked anxiously as she handed him some of the clean bowls for the food, and began to pour milk into the rest.

'They're wild,' Ivo pointed out. 'They'll forage for themselves then be back when the river's gone down.'

'I hope you're right. Trust this to happen while I'm in charge! I'm normally a bit accident-prone, but nothing seems to have gone right since I came here.'

'So I've noticed, but I don't think you can be held responsible for a freak flood.'

'I depend on you repeating those few kind words to your mother when she asks what's happened to all her cats,' Tamsin said soulfully. 'She's bound to phone today to find out how things are going.'

'She won't get through. The phone's dead as well.'

'Oh, great! Next you'll be telling me the hill's sinking.'

Ivo laughed, and she felt ridiculously pleased to have amused him, as pleased as when they'd exchanged that friendly smile outside the barn. 'I've got a personal phone, so that's no problem,' he told her. 'I've already phoned the local police to say we're OK and have enough supplies to hold out until the water goes down.'

'You have been busy. What time did you get up?'

'A little after five.'

'You were going to leave before I came downstairs, weren't you?' she asked a little shyly.

'It seemed the sane thing to do.' Ivo took her elbow and steered her to a bale of straw, where they sat down side by side. When they were settled and still, the cats jumped down from their hiding-places and began to feed.

Tamsin studied them carefully, following Mrs Durand's instructions to look out for any sign of injury or illness. But all the time she was conscious that, for the time being, the friction between her and Ivo seemed to have vanished. She actually felt comfortable with him, even companionable, and that was pleasanter than she cared to admit.

'They look healthy enough,' she said eventually as the cats began to leave their bowls and stalk outside. 'That's a relief. I'm not sure whether a sick cat constitutes a call-out emergency for a helicopter.'

'You'd do it, though, if you were worried, wouldn't you?' Ivo asked, looking sideways at her with a slight smile.

'Yes,' Tamsin admitted, very aware that her shoulder was touching his, creating an intimacy that for the time being wasn't the least bit aggressive. She liked the feeling, and could have sat next to him like this indefinitely—but there were the other animals still to see to.

Reluctantly she stood up and began putting the empty bowls in the basket, leaving a couple that were untouched in case other cats appeared after they'd gone. As Ivo took the basket from her she said, 'Your mother told me she doesn't leave them water because they prefer to drink from the horses' trough.'

'They always have, even when I used to look after them when I was a boy.'

'If you've had strays here that long I'm amazed you aren't overrun with cats!' she exclaimed, astonished.

'Once my mother has established that a cat is a stray, she has it neutered, or there'd be an endless supply of unwanted kittens,' Ivo explained. 'She also has them injected against disease. Considering how wild they are, she's far from being the vet's favourite customer.'

Tamsin smiled but said softly, 'She must be a very special woman, your mother.'

'She is.' Ivo added wickedly, 'She's also a Gemini, so we're not all irresponsible.'

'I never said Geminis were irresponsible, although their idea of responsibility might be a bit different from other people's.' Tamsin thought for a moment, then added. 'They can settle down all right, too. Eventually. . .'

'What's wrong with that? You said you're heavily committed to freedom yourself.'

'I am,' Tamsin confirmed. For some reason, she sounded doubtful, so she repeated more forcefully, 'I definitely am!'

'Why do you think I'm threatening it?' Ivo asked, his shrewd eyes looking intently into hers.

'I never said you were!' Tamsin exclaimed with a flicker of alarm, her strong intuition sensing that he hadn't yet got to what was really on his mind.

'You didn't have to. Your panic reaction every time I get close to you says it all for you. Are you really scared of my reputation or do you play frigid with everyone for safety's sake?'

Frigid! The word hung on the air between them, challenging her, and time rolled back for Tamsin. She could see Simeon's devastated face again, hear the deep hurt in his voice when he'd told her, 'There's nothing wrong with me, Tamsin. It's you. You seem normal enough, but deep down you're frigid. That's what's destroyed us, and that's what will destroy every relationship you ever have.'

She hadn't believed him, but here was Ivo, hinting at the same thing, and plenty of other men had called her cold. She'd always dismissed their accusations as wounded male pride because she didn't like shallow physical relationships, but could it possibly be that they were right, and beneath her capacity for normal sexual arousal there was a solid block of ice?

She turned away from Ivo's watchful eyes, afraid of what he might read in her own. Then she tried to hide her dismay by smiling and answering lightly, 'A woman gets used to being called frigid when she doesn't fall panting into a man's arms. I was expecting something more original from you, though.'

'I wonder why?' he asked.

Tamsin didn't know how to answer him. There was no reason, no reason at all, she realised blankly, why she should expect him to be different, especially given his track record. It was just that suddenly, fiercely, she *wanted* him to be different, wanted him to see her as more than just a desirable body.

If he did then maybe she could come to terms with his reputation, be less censorious, more relaxed, even relaxed enough to——

To what? she wondered, aghast, her heart racing with nervous excitement. To find out once and for all whether or not she really was frigid? Ivo, with his earthy, blatant sexuality, could surely provide the answer to that teaser. If she could bring herself to let him. . .

Tamsin stopped her thoughts there, killed them stone-dead, so afraid was she of where they were leading her. She was also afraid of answering Ivo's question, and so she shrugged it off by walking towards the door of the barn and saying breezily, 'Can we leave the third degree until later? We still have the horses to see to—if you're still game to help.'

Ivo strode after her, but he said, 'You're doing it again.'

'Doing what?' she asked apprehensively.

'Shutting me out. You do it every time I get too close to something you don't want to talk about. Why?'

'Oh, I'm an Aquarian, naturally reserved,' she replied, forcing a smile that was almost good enough to be genuine.

'You're not reserved all of the time, and I know exactly when you're avoiding the truth or faking a smile,' he told her forcefully. 'In fact, I wouldn't be surprised if I know you better than you know yourself. In certain areas, anyway.'

Tamsin felt cornered and vulnerable, far more vulnerable than Ivo would ever be. It put her even more heavily back on the defensive, and as they reached the stable block she joked desperately, 'Now there's arrogance for you! I only hope you know as much about mucking out horses as you think you know about me.'

Ivo gave her a long, thoughtful look, but to her intense relief as soon as the stable doors were open he went straight to a huge gelding and started making a great fuss of him. 'Hello, Duke, old fellow,' he said fondly. 'It's been a long time...'

'Your horse, I take it?' Tamsin commented after watching the gelding, his black coat grizzled grey with age, nuzzle him and whinny softly.

'Yes, but he's too old to take my weight any more,' Ivo replied. 'He's been retired for years. He doesn't forget me, though.'

Tamsin couldn't imagine anybody who'd once known Ivo forgetting him, let alone a horse. Somehow, though, the affection between the two of them got to her, and she said with husky reproof, 'You could at least have brought him a treat.'

'What makes you think I haven't?' Ivo dug into his

pocket and fed the horse lumps of sugar. Then he added with a lurking smile in his eyes, 'I don't suppose a lump of sugar would make you this affectionate, Tamsin?'

'No, I'm a bit more exclusive than that,' she replied, making a big show of fussing a bay mare, another retired horse, to disguise the warmth she felt for Ivo because he so obviously still cared for a horse that was no longer of any use to him.

Truly a kindred soul, her heart whispered. No! her head denied. No! No! No!

The smile in his eyes deepened. 'How about champagne, then?' he suggested brazenly. 'There's bound to be a decent bottle in the cellar. Cold, cobwebby and just right for a romantic candle-lit dinner tonight. . .'

'Right now I'd settle for an unromantic bale of straw from the store-room,' Tamsin responded, frantically trying to blink away the picture of a cosy tête-à-tête that his words evoked in her vivid imagination.

The picture persisted, though, overwhelmingly tempting, and it was with quiet desperation that she moved on to stroke the sleek head of Mrs Durand's grey riding mare.

'Tamsin, you have no soul,' Ivo teased.

'No, none at all,' she agreed, wishing she didn't feel so deliciously shivery when he was smiling at her like this. It took a very real effort for her to add, as though she had nothing but horses on her mind, 'Oh, and we need more hay, too. I'll get the headcollars on while you fetch it.'

'I'm glad I have some uses.' Ivo flicked her cheek with a careless finger and headed for the store-room at the end of the stable block.

If it weren't for the physical attraction putting such a strain on their relationship they could be friends,

Tamsin thought wistfully. She liked the idea of that. They would be able to enjoy each other's company without his reputation or her own reluctance for sexual encounters complicating things.

Tamsin hadn't meant to worry about that again, and she distracted herself by tearing her eyes from Ivo's lithe form as he strode away, and forcing herself into the tack-room at the other end of the stable block to get the gear she needed.

She had headcollars on the two mares and was tying them to a rail outside the stables when he came back, carrying on his shoulder a bale of straw she'd have needed a wheelbarrow to shift.

She tried very hard not to admire him as he dropped the bale at her feet. If there was such a thing as an ideal male, Ivo would be it, she thought regretfully. His strongly masculine face, his height, the breadth of his shoulders, the narrowness of his waist and the lean strength of his hips were the stuff that dreams were made of.

At least, the dreams of women who had nothing better to think about, she reproved herself sharply, and yet she couldn't stop herself smiling when he threw her a mocking salute and promised, 'One bale of straw delivered as ordered, ma'am. The hay will be following immediately.'

He could be so entertaining, Ivo, when he chose to be. When he was in a good mood, his charm, his sense of humour and his all-pervasive sexual magnetism made a very potent mix. . .

Again the fears jolted out of her subconscious by Ivo's gibe about frigidity returned to haunt her, so strongly this time that she was unable to summon up the will-power to stop herself from watching him as he walked back to the store-room. She was still standing there when he returned with a bale of hay.

'Any more orders, ma'am?' Ivo asked, his eyes gleaming with amusement, softening her resistance when she needed so much to be strong.

Swallowing hard, Tamsin shook her head and held out Duke's headcollar. 'I thought you'd like to see to your horse yourself.'

'You thought right.' Ivo flashed her a smile that rocked her back on her heels, took the headcollar and went into Duke's stable, rejoining her shortly afterwards to tie the gelding next to the others.

As Tamsin tipped pony-nuts into three buckets and put one in front of each horse, she lectured herself severely on the stupidity of becoming so susceptible to Ivo's visual impact. She couldn't kid herself that the lecture did her much good, apart from distracting her mind for a while.

While the horses were eating she and Ivo took off their jackets and mucked out a stable each, pitching the wet straw into a wheelbarrow. The dry straw they banked against one wall, then emptied the hanging haynets and refilled them with fresh hay ready for when the horses were bedded down that night. Finally they emptied the water buckets and swept the floors.

The third stable they worked on together, and the feeling of companionship that Tamsin found so beguiling deepened. She simply couldn't resist the carefree feeling that stole over her, but she was surprised to find herself singing as though she hadn't a care in the world.

She broke off guiltily in mid-tune. Ivo looked round at her and commented, 'Nice voice, nice tune. Why did you stop?'

'It suddenly occurred to me that I don't have a lot to sing about.'

'Because you're marooned with me?' Ivo hazarded, smiling. 'Am I really that bizarre? I'd take the bolt out of my neck if it would make you feel more comfortable, but my head might fall into your lap.'

Tamsin giggled. Ivo really could be preposterous! Way over the top, larger than life even, but so—so refreshing! He even made her feel irresponsible—her, Tamsin Sinclair!—and perhaps that was why she scooped up a handful of straw and threw it at him.

A demonic light gleamed in his eyes. He threw a handful back, and the next thing straw was flying everywhere. Suddenly their adult years seemed to fall away from them and they were like two kids let out of school, all high spirits and laughter as the straw fight intensified.

Then Tamsin slipped and fell on what was left of the clean straw banked against one wall. 'Got you!' Ivo exclaimed triumphantly, dropping on his knees beside her and burying her in the straw.

Tamsin squealed and rolled into a ball, but Ivo had no pity. He stuffed handfuls of straw down the neck of her sweater and laughed, 'That'll teach you to start something you can't finish.'

'I'll get even with you,' she gasped defiantly. 'You see if I don't!'

'"Mercy" is the word I'm waiting to hear,' he demanded, picking up a whole armful of straw and dumping it over her head.

'Mercy!' Tamsin spluttered, sitting up and holding out the bottom of her sweater so that the straw he'd stuffed down it could fall out. She was so unexpectedly happy that she exclaimed with a guilt she didn't really feel, 'Anybody would think we were a pair of teenagers!'

Ivo sat back on his heels and grinned at her. 'So what? I have a theory that nobody ever really grows up. Not deep down inside.'

Tamsin brushed the straw from her face and retorted, 'You just want to be Peter Pan.'

'Wouldn't you like to be Wendy?' he tempted outrageously, leaning closer to pluck strands of straw from her hair.

'Right now I'm too busy being Girl Friday,' she reminded him, and without thinking reached out to pluck a blade of straw from his dark hair. At that moment he turned his head slightly and her hand brushed against his cheek.

It was an accidental contact, and yet her hand lingered, and suddenly the laughter was wiped away from both their faces. They stared at each other, their childish game forgotten, swamped by the rampaging needs of a man and woman dangerously attracted to each other.

Slowly, his eyes never leaving hers, Ivo took her hand from his cheek and raised it to his lips. Tamsin gasped as his lips pressed into her palm, their imprint sending unbelievably sweet sensations coursing through her body.

She trembled and her heart pounded painfully against her ribs as she read the intent burning in his brown eyes. 'No, Ivo, no,' she whispered, but there was no conviction in her voice and he swept her remorselessly into his arms.

She gasped again as he pressed her down into the straw, wanting to protest but overcome by the sheer power of the magnetism drawing them together.

Then suddenly it was all too treacherously easy to lie helplessly in his arms, oblivious of past or future, her body wantonly glorying in the sensation of the moment as his lips brushed provocatively across hers, tempting, teasing, tasting, until her white teeth caught desperately at his lower lip and nipped gently in mute protest at this most delicious of tortures.

Ivo's mouth closed fiercely over hers, no longer teasing a response from her but demanding it. And what Ivo demanded she was temporarily incapable of refusing as desire flickered like fire between them.

She felt his hands slide down her shoulders and she shuddered with delight as he grasped her full breasts through the thick wool of her sweater. Her own hands slid down the long line of his strong back, massaging the muscles she found and glorying in their rippling power.

She gasped again and flung her head back as his lips explored the curve of her neck and found the nerve throbbing wildly at its base.

More excitement flared through her body and communicated itself to Ivo. He breathed exultantly against her skin, 'Living it is better than writing about it, isn't it, Tamsin?'

For a moment she didn't know what he meant. Then she remembered the opening lines of her short story, remembered him reading them aloud and then using her as a guinea-pig to act them out. Incredibly, he was doing the same thing again!

To Tamsin, there seemed something so cold and calculating about his intention that she felt betrayed. She wanted to cry out in bitter protest, but Ivo's hands were under her sweater, under her thin T-shirt and moving up over her heated flesh to cover her naked breasts.

She bit her lip as he rubbed his strong, rough palms abrasively over her swollen nipples. Her back arched in ecstasy, involuntarily thrusting her breasts harder into his hands, but all the time she knew that Ivo's triumphant remark had broken the spell that had held her entranced.

She also knew from past experience that, if they made love now, part of her would be disappointed—the part that craved perfection and had always been disappointed. The part that Simeon had called frigid. . .

Ivo lowered his head to clasp one of her breasts in his mouth, flicking his tongue across her hardened nipple while his fingers manipulated the nipple of her other breast.

Tamsin groaned in a kind of agonised ecstasy, but her brain was functioning separately to her body again, and her brain wasn't surrendering. She could make herself willing to submit if she wanted to, but it would be by her own choice, a conscious, considered choice. Just as with Simeon, she wasn't going to be overwhelmed by passion.

Not even with Ivo.

Oh, if only she could accept that nothing was ever perfect, and settle for what was available! Then nobody would ever call her frigid again.

Tamsin, her mind and body in a turmoil of conflicting desires, delights and disappointments, was agonising over what to do next when Ivo took the decision away from her.

CHAPTER SIX

Ivo froze, then raised his head and stared at Tamsin as though he'd never seen her before. She stared back, her wide eyes questioning, completely unprepared when he muttered an oath and thrust her away from him.

With an abrupt, dismissive gesture Ivo pulled her sweater down over her naked breasts and stood up. For a moment he looked down at her with moodily tempestuous eyes, then he strode away to the open stable door and leaned against the door frame, his breathing harsh and rapid, his face turned away from her.

He's guessed, Tamsin thought despairingly. He's guessed something's gone wrong for me and I'm not responding as I should. She couldn't think of any other reason why he should make such a superhuman effort to control himself, unless he was no longer getting what he called the right degree of co-operation.

She sat up, her limbs feeling heavy and numb, her hands trembling as she smoothed down her clothes, her eyes watching him warily. She knew that when he recovered, when his breathing evened out, the recriminations would begin.

It was always that way. Men were never able to accept that they'd done or said anything wrong, so that she was always the one who was blamed for the fiasco. It wasn't for nothing that she normally took such care not to get herself into situations like this.

Tamsin shivered as she remembered Ivo telling her so coldly last night that 'your ability to arouse me has dropped below your ability to infuriate me'. She was certain she'd done the same thing again. In the midst of his passionate lovemaking, too! How much more furious he was going to be now. . .

When he finally turned his head to look at her he said flatly, 'I'm sorry, I had to stop it. It would have been a mistake.'

Tamsin's lips parted in amazement. In heaven's name, why, if he hadn't noticed any cooling of her first wild response to him?

He must have guessed the question trembling on her lips, because his mouth twisted as he told her bitterly, 'While you were just a lovely face, a delicious body, you were fair game. Now——' He broke off abruptly and shrugged.

It was a strangely helpless gesture from a man as far from being helpless as Ivo was, and it went straight to Tamsin's wondering heart. She still couldn't quite believe that he had no recriminations to fling at her, so it was with hesitancy that she repeated, 'Now. . .? What's different now, Ivo?'

'I've got to know you too well.'

'Too well for what?' she asked with even greater hesitancy, still half convinced he would suddenly turn on her.

'Too well to go on treating you like just a desirable object—even though I happen to desire you like mad. Crazy, isn't it?' he asked sardonically.

Tamsin swallowed hard, unbelievably moved that he was putting into words the way she wanted him to feel about her. When she could control her voice she said huskily, 'I don't think it's crazy, Ivo. I think it's touching.'

'Touching?' He laughed, but his laughter had a

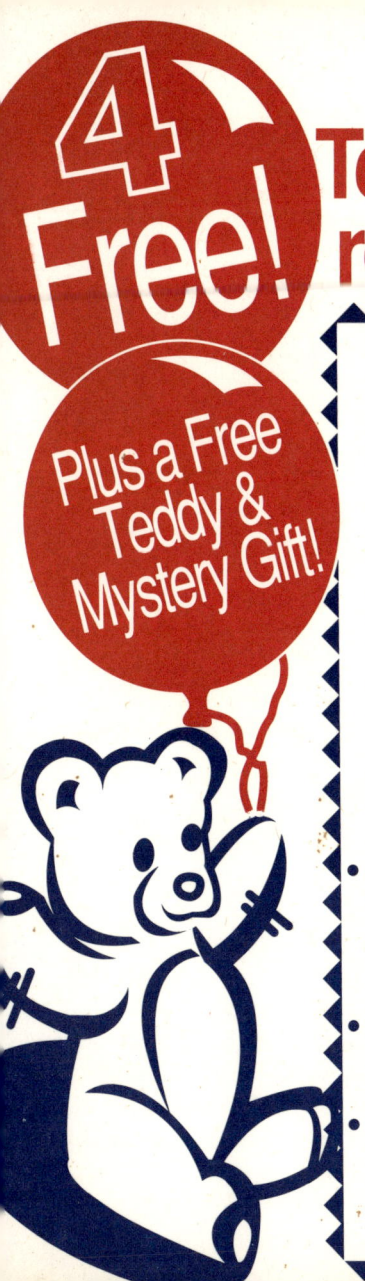

4 Free! Temptation romances

Plus a Free Teddy & Mystery Gift!

In heartbreak and in ecstasy Temptations capture all the bittersweet joys of contemporary romance.

And to introduce to you this powerful and fulfiling series, we'll send you *4 Temptation romances* absolutely **FREE** when you complete and return this card.

We're so confident that you'll enjoy Temptations that we'll also reserve a subscription for you, to our Reader Service, which means that you could enjoy...

- **4 BRAND NEW TEMPTATIONS** - sent direct to you each month (before they're available in the shops).

- **FREE POSTAGE AND PACKING** - we pay all the extras.

- **FREE MONTHLY NEWSLETTER** - packed with special offers, competitions, author news and much more...

Free Books and Gifts claim

Yes Please send me my 4 FREE Temptation romances together with my FREE gifts. Please also reserve a special Reader Service subscription for me. If I decide to subscribe, I will receive 4 superb new Temptations for just £7.00 every month, post and packing FREE. If I decide not to subscribe I shall write to you within 10 days. The FREE books and gifts will be mine to keep. I understand that I am under no obligation whatsoever. I may cancel or suspend my subscription at any time simply by writing to you. I am over 18 years of age.

1A3T

Name _____

Address _____

_____ Postcode _____

Signature _____

Offer expires 30th April 1993. One per household. The right is reserved to refuse an application and change the terms of this offer. Readers overseas and Eire, send for details. Southern Africa write to: Book Services International Ltd. P.O. Box 41654 Craighall Transvaal 2024. You may be mailed with offers from other reputable companies as a result of this application. If you would prefer not to share in this opportunity, please tick box ☐

MPS MAILING PREFERENCE SERVICE

NO STAMP NEEDED

Mills & Boon Reader Service
FREEPOST
P.O. Box 236
Croydon
CR9 9EL

Send NO money now

hollow ring. 'It's not touching, Tamsin, it's infuriating, but, as I said last night, nice girls are hard to walk away from, but walk away I would, sooner or later. I think you call it the Gemini factor. Me, I just call it the way I am.'

'I'm not quarrelling with the way you are if you've come to respect me,' Tamsin breathed. 'That is what you're saying, isn't it?'

Ivo looked at her for a long moment, his expression quite inscrutable, then he looked away again. 'Something like that,' he said.

He sounded almost—evasive. Tamsin was puzzled. Either she'd missed something somewhere, or Ivo wasn't being as honest with her as he seemed. She was afraid to ask any more questions, though, in case they rebounded on her and she had to be honest in her turn.

She didn't think she could be, not completely. She found it difficult to bare her soul to anyone, let alone to a man whose scorn she particularly dreaded.

No, it wouldn't be wise to pry too deeply into what had really gone wrong for him. The questions running around her brain might be difficult to live with, but there was no telling that living with the answers would be any easier.

Somehow, for some reason deeper than any they'd admitted to, she and Ivo had each decided that the other was a no-go area. A kind of mutual rejection, in fact, and it was better by far for both of them to leave it at that.

Ivo had obviously come to the same conclusion, because he eased his lean body away from the doorframe and walked out of her line of vision. As though a spell had been finally broken, Tamsin stood up. She felt a little broken, too, and there seemed no swift way she could put herself together again.

She looked absently at the straw scattered around the stable, and just as absently reached for a broom and swept it back against the wall. She felt as though she were sweeping away all traces of the passion that had erupted so suddenly between them, and she supposed that was the best thing, too.

When she went outside into the breezy sunshine Ivo had just finished stacking the unused straw and hay into an empty stable so that it would be handy the next time it was needed. Tamsin felt a little self-conscious as together they led the horses to the paddock and turned them loose, but she soon realised that her sensitivity was unnecessary.

Ivo had withdrawn into a world of his own, a moody world that deliberately excluded her. She knew she should be relieved, but instead she was shattered by the most searing sensation of loss. She tried to convince herself that if this was the price that had to be paid for non-commitment, for freedom, then she should pay it willingly—just as Ivo was prepared to.

But eventually she had to admit to herself that perhaps she wasn't quite as strong as Ivo, because his silence *hurt*. She didn't like being shut out, not altogether. Besides, between two reasonable adults, surely the fact that they'd deliberately rejected being lovers didn't exclude them from being friends?

Impulsively she put a hand on his arm and said, 'Ivo. . .'

Her voice died in her throat as he shook off her hand as though it had stung him. 'Keep your hands to yourself,' he snarled. 'If there's any physical contact between us we'll be rolling in the grass as surely as we were rolling in the hay. And if that happens it will be on your conscience, not mine, because you've been well and truly warned.'

Tamsin was still so emotionally vulnerable that his brutal rebuttal of her bid for friendship caused tears to choke her throat. She swallowed painfully, then fought back, 'All right, point taken, but you don't have to be so violent about it!'

'Yes, I do!' Ivo exclaimed savagely, his bitterness lashing out at her like a live thing so that she instinctively recoiled. She tried to hide her dismay, but Ivo must have seen how upset she was because he added incredulously, 'You really still don't understand, do you?'

'Understand what?' she faltered.

'That you and I are on the brink of an affair, and it wouldn't work out between people like us. That's why I ended it, before it got started. I've no intention of letting my emotions run away with my life, any more than you have. We're agreed on that, aren't we?'

Tamsin was no longer certain about anything, but she stuttered automatically, 'Y-yes.'

'Good, then we can fight this thing together,' Ivo replied with savage satisfaction. 'We'll start by keeping our hands to ourselves. With any luck, we'll get so sick of being stranded together over the next few days that the whole thing will die a natural death.' Then he turned on his heel and left her.

As Tamsin followed him slowly back to the house she felt emotionally shell-shocked. Everything that had happened between her and Ivo since last night had occurred at such a frantic pace that she needed time to herself, time to reflect, time to recover. And time wasn't a commodity she was likely to have much of, not with so many things needing to be done in the aftermath of the gale.

Guiltily she thought of Mrs Durand's plants in the damaged conservatory. Finding another place for them would be her first priority, just as soon as she'd changed out of her stable clothes.

There was no sign of Ivo when she entered the porch but his jacket was hanging on its peg. It was like a self-betrayal, but Tamsin couldn't stop her fingers touching it, almost caressing it, before she managed to pull herself together and shed her own jacket and boots.

She'd never catch Ivo doing anything half so soppy as caressing anything of hers, she scolded herself as she checked the fridges then went up to her room. He didn't have a sentimental bone in his body.

Tamsin shook her head, trying to dislodge Ivo from her mind as she stripped off and showered, but it was impossible. Her body still retained the glow of his arousing hands, still wanted more.

But there wouldn't be any more. For what it was worth, she'd had her chance and lost it. So had Ivo. Was that really her and Ivo's fault? Or did the fault go back further, to Simeon and to some reason buried in Ivo's past?

Stop it! Tamsin almost screamed to herself as she switched off the shower tap. Stop the post-mortem! No love has died here. No love was even wanted here.

But I'm hurting all the same, she thought despairingly.

When she went downstairs a few minutes later she was wearing a stylish but workmanlike navy jumpsuit with a deep neckline and a scarlet chiffon scarf tied around the elasticated waist. Her brushed but still damp hair fell loosely to her shoulders and she looked her old self again, cool and aloof, with all traces of emotional turmoil studiously banished from her face.

Her nerves jumped a little when the sound of glass being swept up warned her that Ivo was in the conservatory, but she forced herself to continue. Big house though it was, she couldn't avoid him for long, and trying to delay facing him again would only increase the awkwardness she felt.

She threaded her way through the plants Ivo had moved into the dining-room and stood in the open doorway of the conservatory. He'd swept the glass into a pile and was kneeling with a dustpan in one hand and a brush in the other to gather up the shards and tip them into a cardboard box.

His back was towards her and she noticed for the first time how his short dark hair exposed his powerful neck. He hadn't changed, and there was a piece of straw caught in the neck-band of his sweater. She yearned to pluck it away but she didn't dare.

Tamsin waited until he'd tipped another panful of broken glass into the box, then she said softly, 'I should be doing that. Me Girl Friday, remember?'

Ivo turned his head and looked at her. It was a comprehensive look, travelling from her smooth fair hair, down the length of her shapely body, and finally ending at her navy-blue trainers. 'I'll thank you to stay out of here,' he said.

His curt dismissal stabbed at Tamsin's heart. Not only did he not want her to touch him, but he also didn't want her anywhere near him, either.

'You're far too accident-prone,' he went on, standing up and facing her. 'Glass I can cope with. Blood's trickier.'

Tamsin's spirits lifted. Ivo wasn't being hateful, he

was protecting her. Somehow, she couldn't disapprove of the warm glow that spread through her, although she felt guilty enough about it to transfer her attention from Ivo to the conservatory.

She was amazed to see the damage wasn't anywhere near as extensive as she'd supposed. 'Gosh!' she exclaimed impetuously. 'Now you're clearing up the glass it hardly looks touched, and here was I, thinking we would be lucky if anything was left standing this morning.'

Tamsin's heart skipped a little at how naturally that 'we' had paired them together, but although Ivo shot her a swift look he didn't comment. Instead he said, 'If it had been a modern conservatory with big sheets of glass it would have been a different story, but this one was built with small panes in the last century, so the damage was limited. Another fortunate thing was that the wind was fierce enough to carry most of the tiles over the conservatory and on to the patio, where they did no damage.'

'I can clear those up, anyway,' Tamsin said, eager to help.

'I think you'll find enough to do in the kitchen.'

She pulled a face. 'Kitchens aren't exactly my favourite place, and nothing's de-freezing so fast that it needs immediate attention. I checked the fridges when I came in from the stables.'

Tamsin could have kicked herself for mentioning the stables. For a moment there she and Ivo had been talking naturally, and now she felt awkward again. She waited for him to clam up on her for a second time, but he just shrugged and said mildly, 'I'm not your boss, Tamsin. Do whatever you want to do, so long as you don't damage yourself.'

'...so long as you don't damage yourself...' Did that mean he still had some feeling for her, or that he didn't want to be responsible for her? Tamsin wished that she could ask him, but of course she couldn't. It occurred to her then that the next few days were likely to be full of questions that couldn't be asked and therefore would never be answered.

That would be a form of torture to her enquiring mind, but it would be even more of a torture to all that was feminine about her. Ivo was perceptive enough to realise that, but it seemed that his sense of self-preservation was a sight more efficient at shutting her out than hers was at shutting him out.

She watched as he cleared up the last of the broken glass and found herself wishing that she'd spent less of her life dreaming about perfect relationships, and more of it learning to cope with actual ones. She sighed heavily as she realised it was too late to do anything about it now, at least as far as Ivo was concerned.

'What's the matter?' he asked.

'I never quite seem to be living in the real world,' she confessed, driven to speak the truth by the seething emotions within her. 'I'm always looking for a better world, but I never find it.'

'I know that feeling, too,' Ivo surprised her by replying.

'Oh!' she gasped huskily. 'I thought you might think I'm some kind of a freak. What do you do about it?'

'I keep on looking—just as you will.'

'Yes,' she replied softly, 'but nobody else has ever understood that side of me before. It's such a pity——' She broke off in confusion as shyness overcame her.

'That we met before we were ready for each other?' Ivo guessed, once more slaying her with his ability to pick up her thoughts and feelings. 'Yes, it's a great pity, but that's all the more reason not to get involved. All right, so it might be great for a while, but I've never been in a relationship where both people want to break loose at the same time, so the resentment builds up and the recriminations start. Who needs it? Not me.'

'Nor me, either,' Tamsin said fervently, a violent shudder running through her slender frame as Simeon came forcefully into her mind.

Ivo noticed the shudder, was about to comment, then changed his mind. After a moment or two he said instead, 'Then let's get back to work. October days are short, and there's a lot to be done.'

'Yes, of course,' Tamsin agreed, readily accepting the change of subject. 'Where will I find another cardboard box for the broken tiles?'

'In the potting shed. There might be some spiders in them. If you're scared of them, I'll get you a box. I don't want them killed.'

'I wouldn't dream of killing anything,' she assured him, walking past him to the conservatory door that opened on to the patio and garden. 'Live and let live, that's my motto.'

'You're a girl in a million, Tamsin,' Ivo murmured, a certain quality in his voice she'd never heard before. Her wayward heart began to thump painfully, and she couldn't stop herself glancing questioningly at him over her shoulder.

Their eyes met, then he added drily, 'Forget I ever said that, and I'll forget I ever thought it.'

Tamsin walked out into the big garden with her head in more of a whirl than ever, and she'd almost reached the potting shed before she realised how warm she was.

Then she realised that the ancient wall enclosing the garden created a wind-free sun-trap.

She thought that gales or no gales, floods or no floods, she could easily fall in love with the Durand home. It had just about everything—a lovely old house, stables, paddocks, fields, and a walled garden dreamily scented with herbs and flowers even this late in the year.

What about the man who grew up here? something within her whispered. Could you fall in love with him, too? No! she answered as she sorted out the cardboard boxes in the shed. No!

There was only one spider to be liberated from the box she chose, and when she got back to the patio there was no sign of Ivo in the conservatory.

She smothered the pang of disappointment she felt and set to work, clearing up the broken tiles with far more energy than necessary. She'd just finished when Ivo came round the side of the house and stared up at the roof.

'We're lucky,' he said, and again that 'we' coupling them together did funny things to Tamsin's heart. 'I've inspected all the roof, and the only tiles missing are from that edge section there by the chimney. I can lash a piece of tarpaulin over that until a tiler can get here.'

'Can I help?' she offered eagerly. 'Hold the ladder or something?'

'No, I can cope. You see what damage the rain has done inside the house. The end guest room overlooking the back garden will be the one affected. The guest room on the other side of the passage should be all right, but check it anyway.'

Dismissed again, Tamsin thought, but she felt happier as she went back into the house, perhaps because Ivo had recovered his temper. What really counted, though, was that for the moment the friction between them was buried, and if only they could keep it buried it would help them get through the next few days.

The rain had soaked a wardrobe and a chest of drawers in the end guest room, but they were of natural oak with no polish to spoil. They were also empty, so no clothes had been soaked, which cut down the work-load considerably.

Tamsin opened the window, manoeuvred the chest of drawers in front of it to speed up the drying process, and opened the wardrobe doors so that the inside could air. She was rolling up a soaked rug when Ivo said disapprovingly from right behind her, 'Don't move any more furniture by yourself—call me.'

Tamsin jumped, then turned a face flushed with exertion towards him. She was about to say she could manage perfectly well by herself when one look at his expression made her think better of it. 'Thanks,' she said prettily, as though she were the helpless girl he clearly thought her, 'I'll remember that in future.'

She had her reward when Ivo's face softened. He nodded, then looked up at the ceiling, where there was an ugly damp stain. She followed his gaze and said, 'That's the only real damage. Obviously it will need repainting some time, but everything else should dry out all right. As you can see, part of the main carpet is wet, but the rug soaked up the worst of it and that can dry in the garden.'

'Just as well my mother didn't put you in this room,' Ivo observed. 'Your night would have been even more disturbed than it was.'

Tamsin's nerves jumped a little at his reference to last night, but she managed to reply lightly, 'Which just goes to prove that nothing's ever all bad!'

His eyebrows quirked. 'Are you always such a little ray of sunshine?'

'Ask me that when I'm slamming pots and pans around the kitchen later on,' she invited with a smile.

An answering smile spread across Ivo's rugged face, then he seemed to recollect himself and changed the subject. 'Have you checked the room across the way?'

'No, I haven't got that far yet.'

'Let's have a look now, then. I don't want you shifting furniture while my back's turned.'

How, Tamsin wondered, did Ivo think she coped with stable work if she were as frail as he regarded her? Still, it gave her a nice feeling to know that he was concerned, and she resolved that in future she'd get any real work done while he was safely out of the way.

She rapidly finished rolling up the wet rug, then followed him out into the passage. He was frowning at a small area of damp on the passage ceiling, but when they went into the opposite guest room his frown cleared.

'Untouched,' he said with satisfaction. 'I think I'll go down and give my mother a call now. There's sure to be some news on the TV and radio about gale damage in this area, and she'll be worried if she tries to get through to us and can't.'

'She's bound to be worried about her plants in the conservatory,' Tamsin said anxiously. 'How are we going to save them if there's a sudden frost while the electricity's off? Should we move them into the kitchen, keep the fire going, and hope for the best?'

'Not unless we want to hack our way through the foliage with machetes when we're trying to get from the fire to the sink,' Ivo replied with a grin that made

Tamsin's heart turn over. 'We'll move them into the potting shed. It has a paraffin heater we can light at night to offset any risk of frost.'

'Ivo,' Tamsin said impulsively as at least one of her worries fell from her shoulders, 'it's at times like this when I'm very glad you came home unexpectedly. If I were by myself I think I'd be standing on my head by now.'

'A sight worth driving all this way to see if you happened to be wearing a skirt, which you're not.'

A smile trembled on Tamsin's lips, but she said severely, 'I think that's something else I'd better pretend I didn't hear.'

'While I pretend I didn't say it,' he agreed, his firm lips twisting wryly. 'It's going to be a hell of a long three days, Tamsin.'

'No,' she contradicted softly, 'we're doing fine, Ivo.'

'If you think that then one of us must be doing better than the other,' he retorted caustically, and abruptly left her.

Tamsin wished he wouldn't do that—walk away from her so that there was nothing she could do but sigh into empty space. Still, as she went back into the other guest room to pick up the rug and carry it downstairs, she knew that it was Ivo's attitude that was right, and hers that was suspect.

The problem with me is that I want it all, she realised in a moment of blinding self-revelation. I want Ivo and I want my freedom. He's realistic enough to know it isn't possible, and yet I'm the one who's supposed to be wise. Somehow, I've stopped thinking about tomorrow and started living for today, and I mustn't! I'll only end up disillusioned, just as I was with Simeon.

But Simeon, along with all the traumas her relationship with him had entailed, was disappearing rapidly from her mind, supplanted by the far more forceful—and forbidden—Ivo Durand.

Tamsin was feeling pretty low again as she flung the rug over a line in the garden to dry, then went into the dining-room to check all of Mrs Durand's prized plants for splinters of glass.

'I got through to my mother. She hadn't heard about the gale yet, so I was able to assure her everything's fine before she started worrying.'

It was Ivo, startling her as he strode into the dining-room like a panther on the prowl. Tamsin tried to suppress her fluttery reaction to him by saying with assumed lightness, 'Great, now reassure *me*.'

'You're the one who just said we're doing fine.'

'Yes, and you're the one who obviously didn't agree because you stormed off and left me!' she exclaimed, then turned her back on him, wanting to kick herself for being so indiscreet. She'd meant to keep her attitude towards him light, she truly had, but somehow she hadn't been able to stop her hurt from showing through.

No matter how hard she tried to suppress them, her emotions were running out of control, and that just wasn't her—not cool, controlled Tamsin Sinclair.

What, oh, what was happening to her?

Love is happening to you, whispered her heart.

For a moment Tamsin almost believed it, then her brain objected violently, telling her that she couldn't possibly be in love with a womaniser like Ivo. In spite of the physical way she reacted to him, he still represented everything she abhorred! No, it could only be that her research into the Aquarius-Gemini relationship had brainwashed her into a susceptible frame of mind, that was all.

She wished—she wished so much!—that she could return to her usual self. There was a certain safety in being aloof. There was no safety at all in reacting so positively to anything and everything Ivo cared to do or say.

And he didn't help by picking up on her distress and reaching out to clasp her shoulders comfortingly. The quiver that ran through her slender frame was anything but comforting, and she could only be grateful that her back was towards him so that he couldn't see her face. It enabled her to close her eyes in an anguish of longing that almost had her turning into his arms and burying her head in his strong shoulder.

Just for a moment. Just until she got herself together again...

But, of course, it wasn't possible, and she had to battle with all her natural instincts to stiffen her vulnerable body defensively against him and say through clenched teeth, 'No touching, remember?'

His hands fell away from her shoulders immediately, but Tamsin only felt more tearful than grateful. There's no pleasing me, no pleasing me at all, she thought wretchedly. But how could there be, when pleasure was something they'd deliberately denied themselves, and she wasn't even sure if she was physically capable of it, anyway?

A sigh escaped her, another sign of her emotional turmoil, and Ivo wasn't a man who needed signs. 'I never mean to hurt you, but I keep on doing it,' he said, and she was surprised that he sounded almost as strained as she was. 'I'm afraid I'm not very good at considering other people's feelings—not until it's too late, anyway.'

THE THREAD OF LOVE 111

Other people. . .was that all she was to him, this man who'd said they were in danger of having an affair? If so, the danger couldn't have been very acute.

CHAPTER SEVEN

WITH a monumental effort of will Tamsin managed to wipe every trace of emotion from her face and force herself to turn and face Ivo. She wanted him to think she was as tough and resilient as he was, and so she said, 'That's all right, I'm not very good at considering other people's feelings, either.' Then she promptly spoilt her effect by sighing, 'Or so I'm told.'

Ivo's eyes narrowed. 'I think you've been hurt by somebody other than me, and recently.'

'Not so recently, and I wasn't the one who was hurt, not really,' she denied. Then, because she didn't want to discuss what exactly it was about her break-up with Simeon that still troubled her, she rushed on, 'What's more important is that your mother's plants don't seem to have suffered from the gale, apart from a sliver of glass in a leaf here and there.'

'That's a deliberate change of subject if ever I heard one. You still won't let me get close to you, will you?'

'That's what you want, what we agreed on, isn't it?'

Ivo stiffened. 'Of course. Sorry, I forgot.'

In spite of herself, a rueful smile trembled on her lips. 'Just be thankful you don't get your head bitten off the way I do when I forget.'

He looked at her with an arrested expression. 'Am I that bad?'

'Worse, but I don't notice it so much when I'm busy.'

She was expecting him to smile but he frowned more

heavily than ever, turned away, and snapped, 'Then I won't hold you up any longer.'

Instinctively, forgetting what she'd just been preaching, Tamsin stretched out a hand to catch his arm, wanting to tell him she'd only been teasing. But she was clutching at thin air. Ivo had gone again. Sighing, she carried the plants out into the garden, piled them into a wheelbarrow and trundled them down the long garden to the potting shed.

When she returned for a second load she saw that Ivo had a ladder up at the side of the house and was climbing it with a length of tarpaulin folded over his shoulder. She had a burning desire to stop and watch him, but she couldn't exactly hang around like a love-struck teenager and so she carried on shifting the plants.

Besides, I'm neither love-struck nor a teenager, and a good thing, too, she chided herself, certain that Ivo wouldn't have much patience with either state. Then she sighed again, from her very soul this time, and wished she could stop him invading her thoughts...her whole life...

Tamsin was in the kitchen wiping out the emptied and de-frozen fridge when Ivo came in some time later. She was wearing a butcher's-type apron of red and white stripes over her navy jumpsuit. She'd found it in a drawer when she was looking for more dish-cloths, and she hoped it made her look more efficient then she felt.

'How did it go?' she asked casually, keeping her expression as neutral as Ivo's was.

'The tarpaulin's in place. It will hold against anything but a full gale, and we won't be having another one of those for a while.'

'Thank heavens for that,' Tamsin replied, only too

willing to take his word for it. After all, he'd grown up in this place, so he should know. 'I'm afraid we're out of hot water, but I'm keeping a kettle on the stove if you want to wash.'

'You're learning,' Ivo said, moving across the room to the fire.

'So long as the kettle doesn't boil dry! Life in the old days must have been pretty severe.' Tamsin hesitated a moment, then said awkwardly, 'Er—we forgot to have breakfast.'

'You mean we had other things on our mind,' Ivo replied forthrightly. 'Now that we haven't, is there a chance of being fed?'

'More of a risk, really,' she replied, casting a dubious glance at the stove.

'It's a risk I'll take. I'm starving,' Ivo told her, his face relaxing into a smile.

Tamsin cheered up immediately. She felt she could cope with his good and bad moods now, but she was distinctly edgy when he was in neutral—he just wasn't a neutral sort of man. She confessed, 'I'm starving, too, so I'll throw in a bit of everything and make it a sort of glorified breakfast-cum-lunch.'

'Sounds great,' Ivo commented, taking the steaming kettle off the fire and strolling out of the room with it.

While he was gone Tamsin got busy slicing onions and putting them with sausages and steak in an ovenproof dish, put the dish in the antiquated oven and prepared tomatoes and strips of bacon to add in a few minutes' time. Everything was cooking and she was just closing the oven door after putting in a dish of eggs to bake on the bottom shelf when Ivo came back into the room carrying the kettle in one hand and a brown sweater in the other.

He'd not only washed, he'd changed. He looked so handsome in light brown trousers and matching shirt decorated with epaulettes and patch pockets that Tamsin could feel herself going weak at the knees. 'You look as though you're going on safari,' she said. 'Maybe it would have been more appropriate if I'd cooked over an open fire out in the garden.'

'From the smell coming out of that oven, you're doing fine right here in the kitchen. How long before we eat?' Ivo asked, pulling on his sweater and tousling his hair in the process. A few dark strands fell across his tanned forehead, making her fingers itch to smooth them back.

She was fighting the urge so hard that she didn't register his question until he repeated it. 'Eat?' she echoed vaguely. 'Oh, as soon as I've made some tea, or would you prefer coffee?'

'Tea will be fine, but I'll see to it.'

Tamsin nodded, and if happiness consisted of moments pleasantly shared with somebody special, then the next few minutes would have been one of the highlights of the day as she served up, Ivo made the tea, and they settled down to eat together at the big wooden table.

The food looked and smelled appetising, and if the steak was a little tough, the bacon too crisped up and the eggs baked hard, the sausages and tomatoes had come through fine, and they were both too hungry to pick fault, anyway.

Surprisingly there was no tension to make Tamsin jumpy, and she was so beguiled by the easy companionship existing between them that she risked asking, 'Did your mother wonder how we were getting on together?'

'Yes. I told her OK.'

'Oh.'

'Well, we are, more or less, now that we've got each other sorted out. I told her the animals and plants are fine, too.'

'And your sister and the children?'

'She said Margaret's feeling better now that she's there, and the children will soon be on the mend.'

'Good.' Tamsin hesitated, then added, 'I used your phone to call my sister and tell her about being marooned here.'

'What did she say about me being here?' he asked drily.

Tamsin flushed a little. 'I thought it better not to mention that. She knows I'm rather off men at the moment, and I didn't want her to think she's caused me more hassle than she already has. Anyway, the parents of the girl who's replacing me live in Ipswich, so she's driving up to stay with them. That means she'll be close by and can come straight here when the bridge is usable.'

'That's handy,' he commented non-committally, then added, 'This meal is delicious.'

'Thank you, but the truth is that old stove and I fought each other to a standstill. With any luck, I'll improve with practice.'

'You've done very well.' Ivo put down his knife and fork. 'I really needed that meal.'

'So did I,' she replied, wishing she didn't feel quite so pleased with his praise. 'I'll clear away, then, and get on with the next job before all this domesticity starts driving me up the wall.'

Ivo smiled but said, 'The clearing up can wait. We'll relax by the fire while our meal settles, then we'll tidy up together.'

The prospect was very tempting, but Tamsin

demurred, 'I don't think I could relax without clearing the table first. On the other hand, I don't mind leaving the washing-up once it's stacked tidily.'

'The great British compromise,' Ivo murmured. 'All right, let's get to it.'

It gave Tamsin a very peculiar feeling being involved in anything so domestic with Ivo, perhaps because it didn't fit in with the image she had of him, but even more because they seemed so much of a couple. The feeling was enhanced a short time later when they were relaxing in the easy chairs on either side of the fire.

'Comfortable?' Ivo asked, stretching out his long legs so that his feet accidentally brushed against hers.

Tamsin carefully moved hers away an inch before she answered blissfully, 'Mmm... I doubt if you'll be able to shift me for a good half-hour.'

'I won't even try. You've had a short night's sleep and a long morning's work.'

'You, too,' she pointed out, yawning and closing her weary eyes. One moment she was smiling apologetically at him as she yawned again, and the next moment she was fast asleep. It seemed only a few minutes later that she was awake again, but she'd had the strangest dream.

Ivo had been tucking a blanket over her, and pushing her soft hair away from her face. His hand had brushed her cheek lightly and, with wistful yearning, she'd turned her head to press her lips into his palm. Vaguely, mistily, she'd seen an expression of extraordinary tenderness come over his face, then he'd bent his head and kissed her forehead.

Tamsin, coming more fully awake, was shaken by the depth of feeling left by the dream and she looked guiltily across to Ivo. He wasn't there, so she stayed as she was for a while, trying to figure out how a dream could leave her with such a tender, loving feeling.

Then her eyes drifted to the clock on the mantelpiece and she stiffened with shock. She'd been asleep for over an hour. There was still so much she had to do as well! She went to stand up and found that she was wrapped in a blanket.

Ivo! So that part of the dream had been real. What about the rest? Colour flooded Tamsin's cheeks as she wondered if she'd really kissed his hand in that loving way, and whether he'd responded by kissing her forehead so tenderly.

Of course not, she scolded herself. All right, so Ivo had been thoughtful enough to cover her up while she slept, there was no disputing that. But the rest of it—the touching, the kissing, the tenderness—must have been nothing more than a dream settling on a small incident and spinning it into a delightful fantasy.

It must have been a very convincing dream, though, for its emotion to have survived into consciousness, so that she felt almost—loved.

Tamsin sighed and wondered where Ivo was. She was filled with the wildest longing to be with him again, but she could scarcely go and search for him without a good reason. Especially as her next task, emptying the freezer, meant that she didn't have to leave the kitchen.

Restless, racking her brains for some convincing reason why she should consult him, Tamsin prowled around the kitchen until she noticed the dishes waiting to be washed up. She'd forgotten all about them.

Half distracted, she ran the hot tap, but only cold water came out. Of course, the power was off. She'd forgotten about that, too. Now she'd have to fill another kettle and wait for it to heat, when all the time every fibre of her being was yearning to be with Ivo again.

She tried to fight the feeling, but when her eyes fell on the teapot waiting to be emptied she realised she was staring right at her reason for going to search out Ivo. Nothing was more innocent and natural than the offer of tea, and he was bound to be ready for a cup by now. She certainly was herself.

Tamsin put on a kettle to boil and hurried out of the kitchen, pausing by a mirror in the passage to check her appearance. She was used to looking rather soulful and dreamy-eyed, as though her mind was never quite where it should be, but right now she actually looked as though she'd strayed into the enchanted, perfect world she'd been seeking all her life and never found.

Which was ridiculous! she lectured her reflection severely. She was an adult; she couldn't run around looking like a starry-eyed child because she'd found a reason to be with Ivo again. He'd think she'd really flipped her lid!

Besides, once she saw him again, she'd probably find disenchantment had set in and her longing for him had no more substance than her dream.

Smoothing down sleep-ruffled strands of hair with her fingers, she moved on through the house, calling him and getting no answer. Finally she tapped on his bedroom door, very lightly in case he'd also fallen asleep. Heaven knew, he was entitled to! Again there was no answer, so she peeped in cautiously. He wasn't there.

Well, he couldn't be far, not with the place surrounded by water, Tamsin told herself as she went back downstairs. She went through the kitchen to the porch, saw that his jacket was missing from its peg and wondered if he'd gone to see his old horse.

She shrugged herself into her own jacket and was grateful for it when she got outside, because the late-autumn sun had vanished behind low clouds and there was a keen edge to the wind. She walked briskly past the old farm outbuildings, and as she rounded the barn she saw Ivo immediately.

He had a camera looped around his neck and he was sitting on one of the paddock gates, staring moodily down the gentle slope of the hill to the flooded river.

He turned his head, saw her and swivelled slightly on the gate to watch her as she approached, her hands dug deep in her jacket pockets, the wind whipping her fair hair about her face. He lifted the camera to his eye and snapped her, and kept on snapping until she stopped a few feet from him, protesting laughingly, 'Hey, I'm not a model!'

'I know. You never pose. That's one of the things I find so...refreshing about you,' he replied, seeming to choose his words with care.

'Oh,' Tamsin said uncertainly. She was dying to ask what the other things were, but thought better of it. She felt complete, happy even, now that she was close to him again. She moved closer still, leaning against the gate and reluctantly transferring her gaze from him to the floodwater.

'The river doesn't look as angry as it did,' she observed.

'It isn't. The level of the water is dropping, too.'

'Then we might be able to get away sooner than we thought?' she asked, and was shocked by the dismay that filled her.

'Perhaps tomorrow if the water keeps dropping at its

present rate.' Ivo paused and looked up at the darkening sky. 'It all depends on whether those storm clouds pass over. More rain and the river could rise again.'

Tamsin didn't answer. She couldn't. Now she knew why she was so dismayed. It was because, in spite of all she knew about Ivo, and in spite of her determination not to get involved with him, she couldn't quite bear to let him go. After the next quarrel they had, perhaps, but not yet...please, not yet!

It was with great difficulty that she managed to say, 'You must be pleased about that.'

'Yes.'

Tamsin wished he hadn't been so brutally blunt. It wouldn't have hurt him to sugar the pill a little by at least pretending that he wasn't quite as eager to get away from her as he was.

'Why did you take those pictures of me?' she asked, hoping that he'd say he wanted a memento of their time together.

'I'm so bored that I'm shooting anything that moves, and you moved.'

'Thanks very much,' she retorted, hurt as well as offended. 'It's good to know that I'm such scintillating company.'

Ivo caught her face between his strong hands and turned it up towards his, his dark eyes searching hers. 'I've upset you again,' he said, sounding surprised.

'I can't think why!' she retorted, her sarcasm deepening. 'Here was I, coming out to thank you for covering me up when I fell asleep, and now you sound as though you'd much rather have smothered me!'

Ivo let her face go and looked away. 'Not smothered, Tamsin—kissed. I'm not made of iron. Why the blazes do you think I'm out here in such a foul mood, anyway?'

'Oh!' Tamsin's face flamed as an entirely different emotion swept through her, and she stuttered, 'In th-that case, would you l-like a cup of tea? I—I'm just making one.'

'Why the hell do you always behave as though we're on some kind of picnic?' he exploded, jumping down from the gate. 'Why not make it easier on us both by being a first-class bitch like most other women I know?'

He stalked back towards the house and, stung by the unfairness of his attack, she shouted after him, 'I don't know about first-class bitches, Ivo, but I do know about first-class bastards—and you're one of them!'

Ivo just kept on walking. She stared after him, seething. How could she possibly, even for a moment, have wanted to be close to him again? And how could she keep on degrading herself by acting as peacemaker when peace was obviously the last thing he wanted?

She was so agitated that she flung away from the gate, walked down to the river's edge and stared at it every bit as moodily as Ivo had been doing when she'd disturbed him. Disturbed! she mocked herself bitterly. If either of them had been disturbed, it was herself! She'd been permanently disturbed ever since she'd met the man...

Little by little, though, her defensive anger crumbled, and she began to feel so vulnerable that she lingered on by the river, reluctant to give Ivo the chance to trample all over her feelings again.

Eventually the coldness of the wind chilled her right through, forcing her back to the house. Her footsteps dragged and she thought of the overwhelming urge to be with Ivo that had driven her outside in the first place. He, in his own inimitable way, had reduced that urge to the dull ache now throbbing somewhere in the region of her heart.

She checked involuntarily when she saw Ivo in the kitchen, pride straightening her shoulders and lifting her chin defiantly. 'If you're spoiling for another round, forget it,' she said crisply. 'I've got better things to do than indulge in pointless bickering.'

'We don't bicker, Tamsin,' he told her grimly, 'we go straight for the jugular every time.'

Then how come I'm the only one who's bleeding? she thought plaintively as he went on, 'The kettle was boiling when I came in, so I've made the tea. I'm taking mine with me. I've got some reading to catch up on.'

Tamsin watched him leave the kitchen and wondered bitterly what had happened to his offer to share the washing-up with her—vanished into thin air, presumably, like the hauntingly tender feeling bequeathed her by her dream.

But when she went over to the long range of kitchen units she saw that the washing-up had been done and a cup had been set out for her own tea. She shook her head, as perplexed as ever by the multitude of contradictions that made up the complex character of Ivo Durand.

Yet another sigh escaped her as she poured and drank her tea, then she put on the striped apron and set about sorting out the freezer. She was so deeply absorbed in her thoughts of Ivo that without any conscious effort on her part she found the job was finished, which only proved to her yet again the power Ivo had over her mind and body—even when he wasn't around.

She was actually beginning to understand fully the mesmeric fascination that had drawn so many women to him, women she'd formerly dismissed contemptuously as fools.

And here she was, teetering on the brink of being yet another fool, except that in her case Ivo had rejected her as forcefully as she'd originally rejected him. That made her lucky—didn't it?

Yes, of course it did, she told herself fiercely. Ivo wouldn't be controllable until he met a woman who exerted an equally mesmeric fascination over him, and that clearly wasn't herself or he wouldn't turn on her so brutally. He'd feel entirely different emotions, and the main one would be tenderness, the sort of tenderness that he was only capable of in her dreams. . .

Tamsin felt an inexpressible sadness, but that only made her exasperated with herself because a man like Ivo wasn't worth a moment's heartache! She was trying to convince herself of that when a sudden spattering of rain against the windows jerked her out of her mood of brooding introspection. As Tamsin looked towards the windows the brief, exploratory spatter turned into an outright downpour.

She ran out of the house, gasped as the cold rain lashed her, and charged towards the paddock where the horses were grazing. Mrs Durand's instructions had been specific on one point—the two retired horses suffered from arthritis and mustn't be left out if it rained heavily.

She didn't stop to get the headcollars but called the horses as she undid the paddock gate, trusting that their natural instinct would make them follow her back to their dry, comfortable stables.

She was running to open the stable doors, head down against the torrential rain, and would have run straight into Ivo's bulky, weatherproofed form if he hadn't put out his hands to catch her by the shoulders. 'What the hell do you think you're doing, coming out here without any protective clothing on?' he demanded furiously.

She turned her startled face up to his, blinking rapidly as rain hammered into her big blue eyes. 'There wasn't time,' she gasped. 'I have to get the horses under cover. Your mother said——'

'Whatever she said, she didn't intend you to get pneumonia! The horses won't melt for a bit of rain.'

'Neither will I, and I'm not arthritic!'

'You soon will be, if you charge around much longer like this. Stay there!' he ordered, opening the nearest stable door and thrusting her inside.

She opened her mouth to argue when almost immediately Margaret's retired mare came trotting in. Tamsin saw how wet the mare was, took a deep breath and plunged out into the rain again, intending to make a quick dash for the tack-room.

She came out in front of Ivo, who was going in the same direction. She tried to sprint ahead of him but he caught hold of her by the collar of her jumpsuit, bringing her up short. 'Let go!' she yelled indignantly. 'The horses are soaked. I need to get a sweat scraper.'

'What you need is a lesson in doing what you're told to do,' he thundered, 'and I'm just the man to give it to you.'

He pulled her roughly into his arms, jerked her face up to his and kissed her savagely. Pounding rain, shock, outrage—Tamsin was conscious of all these things, but most of all she was conscious of the smell and taste of Ivo as his lips ruthlessly plundered hers.

Then everything faded as her body responded wildly to the brutal dominance of his, and she was weakening with desire when suddenly he thrust her away from him and almost threw her back into the shelter of the stable.

'Now do as you're told,' he told her, his breath rasping unevenly, exciting her even as he repelled her, 'or you know what to expect.'

He left her, and Tamsin stumbled further into the stable, coming to rest weakly against one of the walls. She was so confused that she could scarcely register what had happened, and wouldn't have believed it, anyway, if it hadn't been for her shattered nerves and trembling body.

Before she could recover, Ivo was back again, thrusting the scraper she'd started to go in search of into her hand, and commanding, 'As soon as you've finished drying the mare, go back to the house and get yourself dry. I'll see to everything else that needs doing here.'

'You brute,' she whispered. 'You absolute, awful brute.'

Ivo's lips twisted into an ugly line. 'I don't beat women,' he rasped. 'I kiss them into line.'

'Brute,' she whispered again, but Ivo was striding arrogantly away. Furiously she tried to dismiss him from her mind as thoroughly as he could dismiss her from his, but she didn't have the knack. She couldn't even stop herself trembling so convulsively that it was all she could do to run the scraper firmly over the mare to squeeze the rain from her coat.

It seemed to take her an extraordinarily long time to get the simple job done, and she really had to force some vigour into her arm when she began to rub the mare all over with a handful of straw. Ivo seemed to have drained every last ounce of energy out of her, so that all she wanted to do was run into the house and hide from him.

She made herself stay, though, until she was certain the horse was cared for to the best of her ability, automatically murmuring soothing words of comfort to the mare as she finished the drying process, all the time wishing she had somebody to murmur soothing words of comfort to herself.

Someone like Ivo? Her lips compressed wryly at the thought, and then she froze as she heard his deep voice say from behind her, 'What are you still doing here? You should have been in the house long ago.'

Soothing words of comfort, she thought with an almost hysterical urge to laugh, but she made a monumental effort to get herself under control and said, 'I knew I could depend on you to say something nice.'

She'd meant to speak sarcastically, but to her horror she realised she'd only sounded forlorn, and the face she turned towards him was very white.

Ivo swore savagely under his breath, lifted her up in his arms and strode out of the stable with her. He kicked the door shut behind him, held her effortlessly with one arm as he shot the bolt home, then strode through the driving rain with her to the house.

He dumped her down in front of the kitchen fire, threw off his streaming Barbour and left her as he strode from the room. Tamsin just stood there, frozen as much with shock as the coldness of the rain as it permeated her clothes and chilled her shivering body.

The heat of the fire was welcome, she knew that, but it was all she seemed capable of knowing right then. She stared at the glowing coals as though her whole being was concentrated on the comfort they offered, and was scarcely aware of Ivo when he returned with two big bath towels.

'Out of those wet clothes,' he ordered.

'If you'll turn your back,' she began with an aloofness she would have recognised yesterday but which vaguely surprised her today.

'Don't be such a prude,' he snapped, whipping off her apron and beginning to unbutton her jumpsuit. 'You're soaked and frozen. If you think I'm going to kiss you again, forget it. Right now you look about as attractive as a drowned rat.'

'I d-don't care how I l-look, it's how I f-feel that m-matters,' Tamsin told him, meaning to sound even more aloof but unable to stop her teeth from chattering as convulsive shivers wracked her body.

Ivo swore again, loudly this time, and began to strip her in earnest. 'How d-dare you?' Tamsin protested as he stripped the jumpsuit from her shoulders and arms and knelt to take her trainers and socks off and lift her feet out of her trousers.

For all the notice he took of her protest, she might just as well have held her breath. He rose to his feet and slipped the straps of her scanty lace and satin bra from her shoulders. Instinctively, her arms came protectively across her full breasts, but Ivo only surveyed her sardonically. 'What do you think you've got that's different from any other woman?' he asked. 'Once you've seen one body, you've seen them all, and we both know I've seen plenty in my time.'

Tamsin felt a flare of rebellion at this shameless admittance of his dissolute ways, but he sounded so dispassionate that she also felt foolish—yes, and prudish, too, just as he'd called her. She bit her lip, let her arms fall helplessly at her sides and tried not to feel naked as her bra joined her pile of wet clothing on the floor.

All the same, her hands came down on his as he

began to slip her panties over her hips. 'No,' she said, desperation edging her protest with firmness. Already near-naked, she felt vulnerable enough, and her nipples were betraying her by hardening involuntarily as they were exposed to his eyes and touch.

Ivo looked as though he was going to argue, then, to her profound relief, he merely shrugged and picked up one of the bath towels. Her relief was short-lived as he began to rub her dry with what seemed to her unnecessary vigour.

With only the thickness of the terry-towelling between his hands and her vulnerable body, she was forcibly reminded of the ecstasy his lovemaking had aroused in her in the stables. Was he remembering that, too? she wondered, then bit her lip as he whipped the towel away from her body and began to dry her hair with it.

Again, he worked so vigorously that her naked breasts shook, and she felt as though they were swelling so much with desire that she would die if he didn't soon touch them with his experienced hands or mouth. She bit her lip harder still, wondering how much more she could endure before she broke down and thrust herself at him, when he suddenly stopped.

For a moment they stared at each other. A nerve was throbbing at his temple, in time, she was sure, with the throbbing in the pit of her stomach, then he tossed the wet towel aside and wrapped her in a fresh one.

'Stay right there while I get you some dry clothes,' he ordered, and she wondered how he could be so harsh when she was breaking up inside. Didn't he understand her burning need to be clasped against his body, or was this just another example of how infinitely more efficient he was at shutting down his physical emotions?

'And get those panties off while I'm gone,' he added over his shoulder as he strode from the room.

She eyed resentfully the door closing behind him, wriggled out of her panties and, keeping a tight hold on the towel he'd wrapped around her, scooped up her wet clothing and walked over the cold flagstones to drop them in the linen basket.

'Stay right there...' he'd said, but she was incapable of keeping still. She hung his jacket up in the porch then paced around the kitchen, trying desperately to forget the little scene that had just been enacted before the fire, the frowning preoccupation of his rugged face, the single-minded intensity with which he'd tackled his self-appointed task, the arousing pressure of his skilful hands...

Tamsin's thoughts cut off there and she fled back to the fire as she heard him returning. She was standing dutifully on the rug when Ivo entered the kitchen, her tousled hair tumbling down her back, her shoulders straightening as she shot a wary look at him.

While he'd been upstairs he'd changed back into the jeans and sweater he'd been wearing that morning, but his mood hadn't altered. He asked immediately, 'What happened to the wet clothing?'

'It was making the rug damp, so I put it away,' she replied, and felt a little tremor of apprehension as his jaw hardened.

He thrust some clothes at her, and growled, 'Here, get yourself dressed—and if you don't want any more hassle, stop doing your damnedest to antagonise me.'

She antagonise him! Tamsin burned with the injustice of it. The man was almost permanently antagonised! A walking time-bomb, if ever there was one. She was shocked when that thought sent an illicit thrill coursing through her body, quivering from one receptive nerve-ending to another, as though her stormy acquaintance with Ivo had given her a taste for living dangerously.

Confused and horrified, she switched her gaze from Ivo's hard eyes to the outfit he'd brought her, and was baffled by his choice. 'This is hardly suitable,' she said, frowning at the housecoat, panties and slippers. 'I need something practical like jeans and trainers. I still have to give the cats their evening meal and bed down the horses for the night, and you've forgotten a bra.'

'You're confined to the house for the rest of the day. Another soaking on top of the one you've just had won't do you any good. I'll take care of the livestock. As for the bra, I didn't waste time seaching for something you obviously don't need.'

Colour stained Tamsin's cheeks, but before she could voice her indignation he added roughly, 'For the second and last time, get dressed—unless you get a thrill out of flaunting yourself half naked in front of me.'

CHAPTER EIGHT

OF ALL the passionate emotions Ivo could arouse at will within Tamsin, rage was the uppermost as she buttoned herself into her housecoat with shaking fingers.

She wasn't too pleased, either, that the housecoat he'd chosen for her was the most feminine piece of clothing she'd brought with her. Fashioned from wool of the particular shade of blue that matched her eyes, it was lined with a deeper blue silk that felt softly sensual against her body and rustled as she moved. Its tight-fitting bodice and snug waist clung to her lissom curves before falling in soft full folds to her ankles.

What, Tamsin pondered irately, was Ivo trying to do? Make her look as sexy as possible so that he could prove what a strong character he was by resisting her?

Whatever, she wasn't going to risk 'antagonising' him again by overriding his choice and changing into something else. That's what she told herself, but in actual fact she felt mutinous enough not to care how much his resistance was tested. Every single thing about him tested her in one way or another!

She whizzed up to her bedroom to brush her hair to shining smoothness before tying it back with a blue ribbon—a practical touch that was necessary because she had a lot of cooking to do. She was soon back in the kitchen, the one warm room in the house now that cold rain was bringing a foretaste of winter to the old flint and brick house.

The rain...as the significance of it hit Tamsin she

hurried over to the old lattice windows and peered out. The early October dusk was already falling, but she could see the rain lashing the cobbled stable-yard so hard that it was bouncing up again.

There was little hope now of the floodwater dropping below the level of the bridge so that they could get away tomorrow. No wonder Ivo was in such a surly mood! She'd probably have to spend the rest of the evening bearing the brunt of his temper.

Somehow, though, that prospect didn't disturb her as much as their leaving tomorrow would have done. Deep in her bones, she sensed that parting from Ivo would resolve nothing, and that she'd never be completely free from him unless she managed to overcome the magnetism that had bound her to him almost from the start.

Quite how she was going to achieve that, Tamsin didn't know, but she was becoming fatalistically convinced that something would happen to break the spell that had trapped her with him as sure as the flood had done.

None of which is helping to get the chores done, she scolded herself as she rummaged in a drawer to find another apron to replace the soaked striped one. All she came up with was a flimsy frilled pinny, scarcely practical but better, she supposed, than nothing. She tied it around her waist and went resolutely over to the old blackleaded stove.

She was regarding it doubtfully when Ivo, rain streaming from his jacket again, came in with a full coal-scuttle and a box of logs. He set both down on the tiled hearth and said, 'That's enough fuel to keep the fire going until morning.'

Then his eyes flicked over her shapely form in the blue housecoat, the scrap of frilly nonsense that was masquerading as a pinny, and he took an involuntary step towards her. Tamsin caught her breath, but he smartly stepped back again, the glow kindling his dark eyes vanishing so swiftly that she decided she must have imagined it.

His face became so devoid of expression that Tamsin felt it was safe to say, 'Ivo, I'm sorry about the rain. I can understand how being trapped here with me is making you moody.'

She was rewarded with a softening of his expression, and warmth stole over her as he replied, 'I'm not so sure you do, but you're an OK girl, Tamsin.'

'Thanks, but I'm feeling pretty dumb at the moment. I can't figure out how to build up the fire ready for baking.'

'I'll do that for you.' Ivo reached for a lever hanging at the side of the fireplace, fitted it into a groove in the lid over the fire and lifted the lid off. He added more coal, then replaced the lid. 'That's all there is to it, but call me if you need it stoked up again. What are you going to cook?'

'Everything that will spoil if it's not cooked from frozen. What we don't eat the cats can have. I'll bet they end up wishing they could send out for a take-away, too.'

Ivo smiled, but all he said was, 'You'll manage,' and left her. Tamsin wrestled with a feeling of being abandoned again, particularly as she'd hoped he would stay to act as some sort of technical adviser. By the time she'd baked fish cakes, sausage rolls, pasties and meat pies, and boiled various frozen vegetables on top of the fire, she'd developed a pretty good working relationship with the old stove. She was also sick to death of cooking, which she'd always regarded as a necessary evil rather than an art form.

Harassed, she went in search of Ivo and found him in the little parlour she'd adopted for her own use on her arrival here because it was so much cosier than the big family sitting-room. Her typewriter and reference books were set out on a table, and Ivo had kindled a fire in the hearth.

He was sprawled in an armchair, reading, and Tamsin exclaimed, 'Talk about it being all right for some! I hope you've at least seen to the animals while I've been slaving away over that wretched stove.'

'Stop nagging, woman,' Ivo growled. 'The cats have been fed, the horses are bedded down for the night, and the paraffin stove lighted in the potting shed. I came in here to light a fire so we'd have somewhere more comfortable to sit than the kitchen tonight, and got sidetracked by this hocus-pocus you set so much store by.'

He held up one of her astrology research books and she retorted, 'If you think it's hocus-pocus, don't waste your time reading it.'

'Do you really believe in it?' he asked, watching her narrowly.

'I like to keep an open mind about all things.'

'Except me, obviously,' he said drily.

Tamsin ignored the gibe. 'What I *do* know is that some of the bits about Aquarius are amazingly accurate when applied to me.'

'And the Gemini to me?' he questioned sceptically.

'I think so,' Tamsin replied, very much on her dignity now.

'But you only know me in a very second-hand sort of way. Through the scandal sheets.'

'You haven't done anything to give me a different opinion of you.'

'Why the hell should I?'

'Why, indeed?' she replied coolly, although she knew if there was any real caring beneath the way Ivo was attracted to her he'd be doing his damnedest to give her a better impression of himself. 'I didn't come here for an inquisition, just to warn you that dinner will be ready in half an hour.'

She was turning to leave the room when he said, 'Tamsin.'

She checked and looked back. 'Yes?'

'Your gown is rustling as you walk. I like that. It's the silk lining, isn't it?'

Tamsin's heartbeat accelerated so much that she could scarcely breathe. It took her a moment or two before she trusted herself to reply, 'Yes.'

'I thought so. That's why I chose it. I like a woman to look and sound like a woman. Which reminds me, it says in this book that the best way a man can capture an Aquarian woman is to sweep her off her feet.'

Was he toying with her, or serious? Tamsin called his bluff by replying, 'You don't want to sweep me off my feet, though, do you?'

Ivo paused infinitesimally before he answered, 'No.' He snapped the book shut, and the sound was still echoing around the room as he repeated more forcefully, 'No, I don't.'

Their evening meal was a curious affair, not because it was a hotchpotch of whatever Tamsin had found in the larder or freezer to cook, but because Ivo was trying hard to be non-provocative.

It was so unlike him that it made her uncomfortable.

Somehow, it was less wearing when they were at each other's throats than when they were being unnaturally courteous to each other like this. Last night it would have been natural enough if they'd behaved like strangers forced by circumstance into an embarrassing intimacy—but not today, not after so much had happened between them.

It was all so unreal to Tamsin that long before the meal ended she decided that Ivo on his best behaviour was twice as unnerving as when he was at his arrogant worst.

As she swallowed the tinned asparagus soup, fought with the tough chicken, and toyed with strawberries that had lost much of their flavour in the flan she'd made, she kept asking herself, *why*? Why was Ivo suddenly being so civilised?

Even more puzzling was that she was missing the excitement of the untamed Ivo, who raged and kissed and caressed without giving a damn what she or anyone else thought about him. At least she'd been close to the real man then, she thought wistfully. Now that he was deliberately blocking out all natural responses to her, something deep within her that had just begun to live felt as though it was dying.

She grew quieter and quieter and tried not to think of the candle-lit dinner with a cobwebby bottle of champagne that Ivo had romantically suggested earlier, particularly as he hadn't even bothered to produce an ordinary bottle of wine for the meal.

It all pointed to the fact that he'd stopped reacting to her as positively as she still reacted to him, a feeling that was reinforced later when they were sitting reading before the leaping flames of the fire in the little parlour.

Ivo appeared to have forgotten all about her, and she

did her best to follow his cue. Hard as she tried, though, she couldn't stop herself from stealing quick looks at him. Shameful as it was, she was hungry for the sight of him, far hungrier than she had been for food at dinner.

Her eyes still needed to feast on the dark hair falling over his forehead, the manly, rugged lines of his face, the width of his shoulders, the strength of his arms. It took all her will-power not to stare blatantly at him and pretend, instead, that she was absorbed in her book.

Sometimes she sensed his eyes burning into her, but whenever she looked up he appeared to be reading. Only once or twice did their eyes meet, and then they both immediately looked away.

The minutes ticked into an hour or more, and the silence was so palpable that it was like a third presence in the cosy room. When Ivo finally spoke it was so sudden and unexpected that she almost dropped her book.

'You said yesterday that you're not a very physical sort of person. What did you mean?' he demanded.

The question seemed forced out of him, and Tamsin was surprised into blurting, 'That I'm a flop at the physical side of a relationship.'

The moment the confession was out, she could have kicked herself for exposing herself to his contempt. Ivo was the most physical of men, and wouldn't understand a girl like her.

'I don't believe that,' he replied bluntly.

Tamsin was surprised again by the conviction in his voice, and found herself in the peculiar position of having to defend something she wished she'd never said. 'You would if—if we'd gone all the way in the stable this morning,' she replied hesitantly.

'I'm the one who stopped that,' he pointed out.

'Yes, but I already knew it wouldn't work. It never does for me.' Tamsin turned her face away from his searching eyes and stared at the fire. 'There's always something that stops me responding as I should. Simeon said it's because I'm frigid.'

'Who the blazes is Simeon?'

Again the question seemed forced out of him, and so roughly that for a startled moment Tamsin thought he was jealous. Then she realised he couldn't possibly be, and the fault was hers for not explaining things properly. 'My—my—ex-partner,' she faltered.

'You mean lover?'

Tamsin nodded, hoping the heat from the fire would explain the blush that was once more creeping along her cheekbones. It was ridiculous to be embarrassed like this, but she'd never discussed her own sexuality—or lack of it—with anyone before, let alone with a man whose opinion had come to mean so much to her.

He wasn't about to let her off the hook, though, demanding peremptorily, 'What went wrong for you with Simeon?'

'I don't know. Nothing should have,' she answered slowly, unaware of the puzzled frown creasing her smooth forehead, or the way her hands were twisting and turning in her lap. 'I'd always avoided physical relationships before because I'd never felt deeply enough about any other boyfriends, but Simeon was different.'

'You mean you loved him?' Ivo asked, and she thought he looked white under his tan. But no, she decided, it must be a trick of the uncertain light cast by the oil lamp and the fire.

Still, she found she was actually welcoming his bluntness now. It was helping her to sort out all the fears she'd shovelled to the back of her mind in the hope that, if only she could bury them deeply enough, they would go away. It had taken Ivo to make her realise that her kind of fears didn't fade, they festered.

'Did you love him?' Ivo demanded again.

'If I did, it couldn't have been enough,' she replied sadly. 'Usually I have to be mentally in tune with a man before I can feel physically drawn to him, but that was no problem with Simeon. I'd known him so long, and we'd got on so well, that I was sure the physical side would work out. I wanted it to. I hated disappointing Simeon, I truly did.'

'He must have disappointed you first.'

His astuteness took Tamsin's breath away. When she could she said, 'Yes, he did, but perhaps I should have been less honest and pretended I felt more than I did. I'm sure other women would have, but I couldn't see the point. I mean, I couldn't have kept it up, and that meant I'd have hurt him more in the long run. He didn't see it that way, though. When I tried to explain that there couldn't be any future in a relationship that wasn't honest he said I thought too much and didn't feel enough.'

Tamsin paused, remembering how the reality of an intimate relationship just hadn't measured up to her dreams, and wondering yet again if it ever would. Then she said in a rush, 'I can't seem to—to let go the way other women can. Perhaps I'm too much of a perfectionist, I don't know, but something always happens to spoil things for me.'

'You're forgetting this morning,' Ivo said sceptically.

'No, even this morning I'd have pulled back if you hadn't. At least, I think I would. It was when you began to act out my story again, the way you did last night. I felt you were mocking me, mocking something that might have been——' She broke off, feeling too awkward to go on.

'Special,' Ivo finished for her, his lips twisting wryly. 'Why do you think I needed to mock you—mock *us*?'

Tamsin's lips parted in tremulous surprise. 'I don't know.'

'Because I could only put the brake on by trivialising the situation,' he told her grimly. 'If we'd made love one of us might have found ourselves in a situation we couldn't walk away from.'

You mean me, she thought, knowing full well that she was the one who couldn't love lightly and walk away. Ivo's love 'em and leave 'em philosophy might work well for him, but it never would for her. In her mind, love and loyalty would always go together.

Crazy, mixed-up me, she thought in bitter self-mockery. I want to live and love freely, but I have these ingrained ideals I've never been able to let go of because it would also mean letting go of my dreams.

She wished she could explain that to him, but she feared his ridicule too much even to dare. Her nails dug deep into the palms of her restless hands when he persisted, 'Would you have been able to walk away from me if we'd made love, Tamsin?'

To save her face, Tamsin knew she would have to lie. Not an outrageously obvious lie—she didn't think she could get away with one of those with Ivo—but a lie that had enough of the truth mixed in with it to be believable.

She took a deep breath, summoned up a smile from somewhere, and replied, 'I wouldn't have put you on a guilt trip, if that's what you mean. I'm still getting over the one Simeon put me on, and it's too horrid to inflict on anybody else.'

Ivo's dark eyes seemed to bore into her very soul, then he said abruptly, 'Would you be able to walk away from a man who could prove to you that you're not frigid?'

Good grief! Tamsin thought. He wants to know whether he can make love to me without getting entangled in another complicated affair. Her pulses jumped in a mixture of excitement and alarm, causing her wayward heart to beat erratically.

She shifted nervously in her chair, not knowing how to answer him, uncomfortably aware that she was being made to face up to things about herself she'd rather not know.

And the most vital of them all was that yes, she did want Ivo to make love to her. Her dream of the perfect, enduring relationship, her revulsion of his scandalous lifestyle, her doubts of her own sexuality, her contempt for shallow encounters—all paled to nothing compared to the burning desire she felt to be in his arms.

She knew she would only find herself there if she accepted him on his own harsh terms. It was a bitter pill to swallow, and yet so overwhelming was her desire for him that she told him what she was certain he wanted to hear.

'After my experiences with Simeon it would be a pleasure to walk away from anyone. That was the hardest part with him, you see. He wanted us to stay together, work at solving our problems, but I found it unbearable to be trapped in a relationship that had lost its meaning. I left him because I had to, but I felt so guilty about it that it made me value my freedom above anything else.'

That used to be the truth, sure enough, but she'd changed so radically in the short time she'd known Ivo that she had to take a deep breath before she plunged on, 'I never want to be trapped like that again, so it will be years—if ever—before I let myself in for another lasting relationship.'

There, somehow she'd managed it, given Ivo permission to make love to her with no strings attached. She'd also managed to preserve a calm façade, but inside she was quivering with tension as she waited for his reaction.

It was slow in coming, so slow that she forced herself to look into his eyes. The burning intentness had gone from them and they were as expressionless as his voice when he finally replied, 'I see.'

And that was all he said. Just 'I see'. Tamsin waited for more, and was completely bewildered when he returned to his book and began reading as though they'd been discussing nothing more startling than the weather.

Gradually, shamefully, Tamsin began to realise that she had misunderstood the situation. Because nothing had killed her desire for him, she'd assumed he still desired her, and so she'd read into his questions meanings that had never been there.

He'd merely been curious about her and she, naïve little dreamer that she was, had been first startled and then beguiled into revealing all those carefully guarded secrets about herself that wild horses wouldn't normally have dragged from her.

Humiliation burned through her as she recollected how she'd more or less offered herself to him, and she didn't know what was worse, the pain of his indifference or the pain of her own humiliation.

Whichever of the two it was, she couldn't blame either on Ivo—only on herself for being such a lovesick fool. *Lovesick*! Fresh torment devastated her as she realised that yes, that was exactly what she was. No other feeling but love—raw, burning love—could have led her to expose herself as thoroughly as she'd just done.

Shame flooded her again, so fiercely that she wanted to get up and rush from the room, but she knew she couldn't possibly do that. No, she had to sit on in the same room with Ivo, trying to assume an indifference that was equal to his, so that she could salvage the only thing that was left to her: her pride.

Tamsin forced herself to open her own book and turn the pages at regular intervals as though the words that were blurring before her eyes actually had some meaning. It was a self-imposed purgatory, and she endured half an hour of it before she closed the book and stood up.

'I think I'll turn in now and get some writing done,' she said, marvelling at how naturally she managed to speak. Who would guess that she was breaking up inside? Not Ivo, thank heaven! But grief, did he have to look at her so intently, as though he actually had a real interest in anything she said or did? It was a farce, considering he'd just proved the very opposite.

'Do you write best at night?' he asked.

'It varies, but this is the first time today my mind's been untangled from domestic stuff. With any luck, an idea or two will flow.'

'Are you still going to abandon the story you've already started?'

'Yes. It—it lacks reality.'

'Whatever it lacks, it isn't reality,' Ivo replied drily. 'We've proved that between the pair of us more than once.'

Tamsin stiffened with outrage. The nerve of the man! Having found out all about her that he wanted to know, he was taunting her now. How could he? Oh, how *could* he? She turned away from him in disgust, grabbed an armful of her research books and stalked towards the door.

The hairs on the back of her neck prickled when Ivo stood up and followed her. She flung a questioning glance back at him and demanded, 'Where are you going?'

'With you, of course,' he replied, picking an oil lamp up from the table. 'Somebody has to light the way for you, or have you forgotten there's no electricity?'

Of course she'd forgotten, so fearful was she of being overwhelmed by her misery before she was alone. 'I can carry the lamp,' she said, but as she reached for it one of her books slid from her arm.

Ivo retrieved it from the floor and gave it back to her. 'No way am I going to let you wander around the house with an oil lamp. Or have you also forgotten that the fire engine can't get over the bridge?' he added satirically.

'Whatever I drop, it won't be the lamp,' she argued fiercely, but Ivo merely cut the argument short by taking her arm and steering her out of the room. He kept hold of her as they walked along the passage, and although his grip was light Tamsin was burningly conscious of it.

No touching, he'd ordered, but presumably that rule still only applied to her. How like Ivo that was! She swallowed her resentment, afraid that if she told him to let go he'd guess that she was still desperately vulnerable to his slightest touch. Her pride demanded that he believed she'd switched off her feelings as easily as he had his.

As they walked up the stairs together the oil lamp gave them a bright area of light but cast everything else into deepest shadow. Somehow it brought the atmosphere of the weathered old house to life, and Tamsin had the curious feeling that they'd slipped back a century in time.

She could imagine Durand men down the ages lighting their wives' way up to bed like this. It would have to be wives, of course, not single women like herself, not unless Ivo's ancestors had ignored the moral standards of their day and carved the same unashamedly scandalous path through life as he had.

'Penny for them,' Ivo said.

Tamsin was startled out of her reverie and almost dropped her books again. She grabbed them to her and replied frankly, 'The atmosphere is getting to me. I was wondering whether your ancestors enjoyed making scandals as much as you do.'

Ivo stopped on the top step, his hand on her arm forcing her to stop, too. 'I don't enjoy scandals and I don't make them,' he told her sardonically. 'It's the women I get involved with who make a speciality of that.'

'And you're just the innocent dupe?' she scoffed, wishing he didn't look so damned handsome by oil light. The wild, untamed air that clung to him even when he was trying to behave in a civilised manner was more pronounced than ever. It teased her senses, stoked her desire for him and tantalised everything that was feminine within her.

What a challenge he was! she thought breathlessly, no longer wondering how he'd managed to slice through her defences so devastatingly. But how dared he blame his reputation on the women he got involved with? Surely only a skilled double-talker could possibly hope to get away with that.

'I don't kiss and tell,' he replied with careless arrogance. 'They do.'

Tamsin drew in her breath in an outraged gasp and asked scathingly, 'That makes everything all right, does it?'

Ivo merely shrugged. 'I'm no saint, but I've never promised a long commitment to any woman. If she can't accept it when an affair is over, that's her hang-up, not mine, and you should understand that better than anybody. You were only just saying how unbearable it is to be trapped in a dead relationship, especially when you're no good at pretending. Why blame me, when you decided for yourself that there's only one thing to do, and that's walk away?'

If not run, Tamsin thought, feeling an unexpected and unwanted surge of sympathy for Ivo. She fought it, and exclaimed, 'You can't compare us! One bad experience was enough for me. You just keep on having them!'

'What do you expect? I'm a man, not a monk,' Ivo growled, beginning to steer her along the upper passage.

'Yes, but if you've never deceived those women, why do they tell their stories to the papers?' she asked.

'Money, publicity, spite—how the hell should I know?'

'Or revenge because you *did* make promises to them that you didn't keep?' she flashed.

Ivo put the oil lamp down on a side-table in the passage and swung her towards him. She gasped and clutched her books across her breasts in desperate defence, but he only grasped her shoulders. Then he looked intently into her eyes and demanded, 'If we had an affair and it didn't work out, would you go to the papers with your story?'

'You know I wouldn't,' she gasped, revolted at the very idea.

'Yes, I know—and I also know that that's because you're not the sort of woman I usually get involved with,' he told her savagely. 'They're publicity-mad models or socialites, and having an affair with me guarantees them a place in the spotlight. That's what they can't live without, not me. I don't break hearts, I build marketable and high-profile reputations.'

Tamsin was stunned by both his cynicism and the insight it gave her into his attitude to women. Then, guiltily, she realised she'd never looked at any of the scandals from his point of view. As a woman, she'd believed what other women had said about him. No wonder he was so cynical! 'But—but you must have known some genuine women,' she faltered.

Ivo's lips twisted bitterly. 'They're the sort I've learned to stay well clear of. They always think they can turn a temporary relationship into a permanent one, and they get spiteful, or tearful, or stick like glue when they don't succeed. I hate it when women fall in love with me. It only complicates things, and it's so unnecessary. On the whole, the kiss-and-tell type are preferable. We understand each other better.'

'Haven't you ever met a woman you'd like to stay with?' Tamsin asked, remembering Ivo in his softer moods and finding it hard to believe that he didn't have a heart somewhere to be won.

He surveyed her enigmatically for long seconds, then released her as abruptly as he'd caught hold of her.

'Apparently not,' he replied, picking up the oil lamp again and striding ahead of her to her room.

Tamsin hurried after him, trying hard to puzzle out what he meant, but he gave her no further clue as he put the oil lamp down on her bedside table and showed no inclination to linger.

As he turned to leave he said, 'I put a torch on your bedside table earlier so that you can find your way to your bathroom. I'll light the lamp in there before I go downstairs, and all you have to do is turn it out before you come back here.'

'Thank you, that's very thoughtful of you,' she replied formally. 'How will you light your way downstairs?'

'I don't need a light. I grew up here. I know my way blindfold.'

He strode towards the door, but she said impulsively, 'Ivo...?'

'Yes?' He turned back towards her, a big shadow now that he was out of range of the oil lamp's glow.

'This is such a lovely old house, and it's your heritage,' she said. 'Will you ever come back here to live one day?'

She sensed rather than saw his face harden, and felt the strangest pain when he replied harshly, 'This house was meant for children, and children need to grow up in a stable environment. That hardly fits in with what you call my scandalous way of life, does it?'

She wanted to cry out against his bitterness, tell him that now she'd heard his side of the story she wasn't as critical as she'd once been, but he gave her no chance. He went out, shut the door firmly on her, and left her alone with her turbulent thoughts, and her even more turbulent emotions.

Tamsin showered, got into bed, and thought how

ironic it all was. She'd thought Simeon, whom she'd got to know slowly over several years of friendship, was the ideal man for her, but she'd been wrong. Then she'd thought Ivo, whom she'd known for no time at all, was the personification of everything she loathed, but she'd been even more wrong about that.

In fact, she seemed to know less about love now than she ever had, but at the same time with Ivo she'd glimpsed the full, unbelievable heights and depths of it. Glimpsed, partially experienced, and then lost.

CHAPTER NINE

TAMSIN awoke with the same need to be close to Ivo that she'd experienced the previous morning, but he did his best to confirm that it was a need he no longer shared. By mid-morning it was obvious he was deliberately avoiding her and, immeasurably hurt, she made it easy for him. She had to, so fearful was she that her hurt would show.

They moved about the lovely old house, doggedly avoiding each other, coming together only for meals, when it seemed to Tamsin that she was alone in experiencing the powerful attraction they'd both once found so hard to resist.

Restless, miserable, she found herself being drawn back time and time again to the river. During the night the rain had stopped, and the level of the floodwater was dropping dramatically. As she searched the sky hopefully for rain clouds it remained obstinately clear. By evening the bridge was visible, and Tamsin stopped hoping.

Tomorrow she and Ivo would go their separate ways, and there was nothing she could do about it. Nothing, although she knew her life would never be the same again.

Much as she'd grown to love the old house during her short stay, staying on without him for only a few hours would tax her sorely. His forceful presence would linger, haunting her at every turn, increasing her anguish, deepening the loss she was already feeling.

She didn't think she could bear it, so as soon as Ivo went into the parlour after dinner she used his phone to contact her sister.

'Hi, Gemma,' she said, trying to sound her normal cheerful self. 'Guess what? The flood's receding! It looks as though I'll be able to get away tomorrow if you can get my replacement organised.'

'I'll get on to it right away,' Gemma replied breezily. 'Her name's Sara Lawley and I'll tell her to be there in the morning.'

'Are you sure she's sound with animals?' Tamsin asked anxiously. Reluctant as she'd been to be pitchforked into this job, it seemed she hadn't been able to avoid getting involved with everything that concerned the Durands—their house, their horses, their stray cats. Ivo. . .

'Sara's as sound as a pound,' Gemma responded. 'She was raised on a smallholding in Dorset. Apart from the flood, you haven't had any problems, have you?'

'No,' Tamsin fibbed, glad that she hadn't revealed Ivo's unexpected arrival. It would only rub salt in her wounds to have to talk about him, even with her sister. For once, her natural reluctance to discuss her feelings had paid off. . .

'Well, thanks a million for helping me out,' Gemma replied. 'How's the story going?'

'It's been a bit difficult to concentrate, but I'll soon lick it into shape once I get home. Well, with any luck I'll see you tomorrow, Gemma. Cheers!'

She hung up hastily as Ivo walked into the kitchen, then said as casually as she could, 'Have you noticed the river's almost back to normal?'

'Yes.'

He didn't sound very pleased about it, but Tamsin

supposed he had doubts about leaving her in charge here, and she didn't really blame him. She hadn't been much more than a walking disaster area ever since he'd arrived.

Anxious to reassure him, she said, 'I've just phoned my sister. My replacement will be here in the morning, if the bridge is usable. I think I'll go up and start packing.'

'You're anxious to get away.'

Now he sounded surly, and Tamsin was surprised into replying, 'Aren't you?' Then she made the mistake of looking directly into his eyes, something she'd carefully avoided doing on the rare occasions she'd seen him that day, and her vulnerable heart began to hammer against her ribs.

It seemed to her that Ivo was looking at her every bit as hungrily as she was trying not to look at him, but that couldn't be right. It couldn't be! Confused, she turned away and told herself fiercely to stop imagining things. She was shaken, though, and there was a slight tremor in her voice as she continued, 'I mean, we haven't exactly been happy castaways, have we?'

'No,' he said flatly, then swung away from her to walk over to the fire. 'I'm making coffee,' he went on. 'Care to join me in a cup?'

It was the first time that he'd actually invited her company all day. Tamsin was desperately tempted, but, fearing she'd betray her feelings if she stayed close to him for too long, she shook her head.

'Maybe later. Right now I'd rather put my things together while I'm in the mood. I'd hate to get back to London and find I've left a book behind or something.'

She managed an uneasy smile, then did her best to walk out of the kitchen as though she hadn't a care in the world. Up in her room, she lit the oil lamp and packed quickly, desperate for something to do, although she knew that if she scrubbed the house from top to bottom she still wouldn't succeed in taking her mind off Ivo.

All too soon the packing was finished, and she was more restless than ever. It wasn't anywhere near her normal bedtime, but she decided another night of tossing and turning in bed would be preferable to the strain of going downstairs and trying to act as though Ivo meant nothing to her.

She grabbed her pyjamas, dressing-gown and torch and went to the bathroom, shuddering through a cold shower rather than risk encountering Ivo by going down for a kettle of hot water to wash with. Teeth chattering, she tried to rub some warmth back into her body with a towel, wishing she'd brought something more substantial than silk to wear to bed. A voluminous neck-to-toe flannel nightie would be more appropriate in this old house when the heating was off.

To blazes with it, she'd sleep in her dressing-gown as well, she decided, putting it on and tying it around her waist as she hurried back along the passage. She stopped in mid-stride and began trembling in earnest when she saw the big, burly shape of Ivo in her bedroom.

'I was wondering where you'd got to,' he said. 'I thought I'd come up to see whether you're ready for that coffee yet. It seems a shame to waste a fresh pot——' He broke off abruptly, his dark eyebrows lowering as he studied her with narrowed eyes.

Tamsin was miserably conscious that her silk nightwear revealed rather than concealed the wild trembling of her body, but she wasn't prepared for the harshness with which he demanded, 'Why the hell are you shivering like that? You're not scared of me, are you?'

'N-no, of course not,' Tamsin stuttered. 'I-I've just had a cold shower, that's all.'

'Silly little fool,' he growled, taking her arm and hustling her back out of the door. 'I'd have brought you up some hot water if you'd asked for it. Back downstairs with you, before you catch your death of cold.'

Tamsin tried to hang back. 'I-I'm fine,' she fibbed. 'I'll soon warm up once I'm in bed.'

'You'll warm up before you go anywhere near that bed,' he ordered, propelling her towards the stairs. 'I'll get you that coffee and a hot-water bottle.'

'But——' she began, still trying to hang back so that he had to either relent or force her along.

Being Ivo, he chose force. Smothering an oath under his breath, he caught her up and carried her effortlessly down the stairs. The moment Tamsin's body felt the warmth and comfort of being in his arms, her fiercely suppressed feelings betrayed her. Her shivering lessened, she stopped protesting, and it took all her will-power not to snuggle up to him.

'You're a devil of a girl for making a fuss about nothing,' he told her as he carried her into the little parlour and bent to put her down in an armchair by the fire. When Tamsin didn't answer he straightened up and challenged, 'Aren't you going to call me a brute? You usually do when you force me to put a stop to your nonsense.'

Tamsin still didn't trust herself to reply. She needed time to adjust to no longer being in his arms, to fight a weakening urge to burst into tears, and so she turned her head away and stared fixedly at the fire.

Ivo only ever took her into his arms when he was

impatient with her or he had some point to prove, and she wanted——Oh, what was the use of dwelling on what she wanted?

Ivo studied her then asked suspiciously, 'Are you sulking?'

'N-no,' she whispered with a betraying tremor.

To her horror, Ivo knelt beside her armchair, thrust a hand under her chin and forced her face round to his. His dark eyes searched hers, then he said in a much softer tone, 'You're upset.'

'No, I'm not,' she replied, turning a suppressed sob into a defiant sniff.

It didn't deceive him for a moment. He released her chin and said with a rough concern that went straight to her suffering heart, 'Yes, you are, and it's all my fault. You're right, I am a brute.'

Tamsin could fight his arrogance and his forceful ways, but she had no defence against his concern. She didn't want him to be nice to her, not now, when it was far too late. She'd fall apart, she knew she would, and so she tried to laugh the whole thing off by replying lightly, 'Well, let's just say that you haven't used much of your famous charm on me.'

'You ordered me not to,' he reminded her. 'You said I wasn't to treat you like one of my women.'

'So I did,' she said with an uncertain laugh, wondering whether she'd been out of her mind at the time. But no, she recollected, she'd still been hanging on to reality then. It was now, now that she knew she loved him, that she was out of her mind.

Ivo got to his feet with one of those abrupt movements that made her feel so rejected. 'I'll get you that hot drink I promised you. Who knows, it might make you think I'm less of a brute. . .'

He looked and sounded so strained, so unlike himself, that Tamsin couldn't bear it. Impulsively she caught his hand as he was turning from her, and said softly, 'I don't think you're a brute, Ivo, not really.'

His face hardened again, and he said harshly, 'Don't be kind to me.'

'Kind?' she repeated with a little shake of her head. 'I'm not trying to be kind, I'm trying to be fair. I don't think it's been possible for either of us to be our normal selves because the circumstances have been so abnormal. A trapped Gemini or a trapped Aquarian isn't exactly passive, and here we've been, the two of us——'

'For heaven's sake, don't start talking about Gemini and Aquarius again,' Ivo broke in hoarsely. 'You'll remind me of the opening lines of your story, and I've been going mad remembering what it was like when I was acting them out with you.'

Tamsin's throat constricted painfully. Ivo—arrogant, contemptuous Ivo—sounded as tormented as she was herself. 'But—but it was only ever acting,' she faltered.

'Was it?' he demanded. 'If that's what you think then it's time I put you right on that score.' He grasped the hand she'd placed on his and pulled her to her feet. Tamsin had just a split-second to read the naked intent in his eyes before she was crushed in his arms and his lips were pillaging hers...

She surrendered to the savage intensity of his kiss without a second thought, or any thought at all. Her heart beat wildly against his, her eyes closed, her body moulded itself to his, and her hands slid up over his shoulders to cling to his neck.

She felt his arms tighten around her soft body, felt his breath hot against her lips as he murmured feverishly,

'Tamsin. . .my darling Tamsin. If only you knew how much I've wanted to kiss you like this.'

She wanted to tell him that she'd felt the same, but the words wouldn't come. She was feeling far too much to speak, overwhelmed by the fierceness of his ardour and the unashamed eagerness of her own response.

All the things that normally distracted her, her doubts, her insecurities, her previous unhappy experiences, were forgotten as Ivo stormed her into a world where sensation was everything. And, if she hadn't already fallen in love with him, she would have loved him now, captivated by the sheer joy of being able to surrender to her own sensuality at last.

'Ivo. . .' she murmured brokenly. Then again, 'Ivo. . .'

He raised his head and looked at her, his eyes dark pools of desire, his hair waving wildly over his forehead, and he seemed to Tamsin so much the idealistic lover of her dreams that her lips parted in tremulous wonder.

'Lord, you're so vulnerable,' he muttered thickly, thrusting her head into his shoulder and holding it there, as though he was fighting to regain self-control. 'I really would be a brute if I took you like this. . .'

Tamsin marvelled that he was the one who was doubting now, and she was the one who was so sure. It filled her with a power she'd never known before, a wonderful power that made her feel completely, gloriously female.

'No, Ivo, I'm not vulnerable,' she denied softly, 'I was, but I'm not any more. I-I want you as much as you want me.'

'Are you sure?' he demanded, his hand tangling in her hair, forcing her head back so that he could read her eyes.

THE THREAD OF LOVE 159

'If I'm not, persuade me,' she tempted him huskily.

Ivo gasped, caught her hand and pressed his lips passionately into her palm. A flicker of heat shot up her arm, making her catch her own breath, and lovingly she kissed his hand, too. She looked up at him from under her eyelashes, and almost stopped breathing as she surprised an expression of unbelievable tenderness in his eyes.

This was an Ivo she'd never seen before, and her heart overflowed with love for him. She thought wonderingly that there were so many different ways to fall in love with a man, and she was discovering a new one every minute—unless it was the same love expanding and growing to fill every corner of her heart, body and soul.

She sighed as he began to brush his lips all over her face, her neck, her shoulders, pausing to press lingering, tantalising kisses on her susceptible skin, then moving on in an unhurried voyage of exploration.

The feelings he aroused in her were so loving, so sublime, as she turned her head this way and that to accommodate his searching lips. She kissed him back whenever she had the chance, and rubbed her cheeks against his in blissful appreciation of the way he'd changed the pace of his lovemaking, leisurely satisfying her need to be loved as a whole woman before she was taken in passion.

When his hands slid down over her silk-clad shoulders to cover her breasts she instinctively arched her back to offer them up to him. She felt first her dressing-gown, then her pyjama jacket slip to the floor, and she gasped as his strong hands closed over her naked flesh, her hardened nipples caught between his fingers.

She gasped again as his fingers closed and opened,

closed and opened, gently squeezing and releasing her nipples in a rhythmic, tantalising fashion that was so ecstatic that it became almost a torture. Her lips parted, fiercely seeking satisfaction from his as an ache that started in the pit of her stomach began to burn through her entire body.

Feverishly she undid his shirt and pressed her taut breasts against the dark hair matting his chest. She rubbed herself against him, finding a temporary relief from her torment, and it was Ivo who gasped and became feverish.

He tore off his shirt and pressed her even more fiercely to his chest, his strong hands moving up and down the length of her slender back, settling over her hips and pressing her hard against his swollen manhood.

Instinctively, Tamsin rubbed her hips against his, her hands clasping his hard buttocks, unable to believe that this wild, demanding creature was really her, unable to believe either that she'd snapped the control of a man as arrogant and sophisticated as Ivo, and turned him into a creature as lustful and primitive as he'd made her.

Untamed, she thought exultantly. And he's mine. Whatever happens later, right here and now he's mine!

That was her last conscious thought as Ivo pulled her down on to the thick, long-piled rug in front of the fire and slid her pyjama trousers down over her thighs and long shapely legs, kissing every inch of flesh he exposed.

Her hands found the waistband of his trousers, undid it, and Ivo helped her to make him as naked as she was herself. Then he began to kiss the whole long line of her lovely body, his lips fastening on each breast in turn, his tongue flicking her nipples to fresh flame.

She flung her head back, her long fair hair spilling

across the rug, as his lips moved down, seeking and arousing the secret parts of her body until she was writhing in the most delicious torment. Just as she felt she could endure no more, he took her, and she clung to him, moving as he moved, her teeth sinking into his shoulder as she sought the satisfaction she craved.

When it finally came she cried out in ecstasy, but Ivo gave an even greater cry as he collapsed against her. Tears trickled down Tamsin's cheeks, helpless tears reflecting the unbelievable joy of what had been a truly consummate union. She felt exhausted, but she also felt reborn, and the love that she felt for this powerful man who now lay temporarily helpless against her was as complete and all consuming as their union had been.

She stroked his hair, murmured incoherent words, and felt fresh joy as he tenderly kissed away her happy tears. He was still hers, then, for the moment.

It was enough for Tamsin and she closed her eyes, smiling sleepily as he pulled a fur wrap from one of the chairs and covered them with it. The only thing she needed now was for him to snuggle down with her, and he did, lifting her into his arms, cradling her head against his shoulder, and smoothing her hair back from her face as she hovered blissfully on the borderline between consciousness and sleep.

'Tamsin. . .' he said softly, and it seemed to her that there was a trace of anxiety in his deep voice.

Tamsin didn't want to know about anxiety, not now, when everything was so perfect. 'Ssh,' she whispered, 'Ssh. . .'

Tomorrow she would tell him it was all right, he didn't have to worry, she wouldn't try to hang on to him or make any kind of fuss. She couldn't even if she wanted to, because she loved him far too much to make him unhappy.

She wouldn't tell him that, though. Seconds later she was completely asleep, and in her sleep she sighed. Ivo, looking down at her, frowned. As her face softened, his hardened, and it was hours before he slept.

Tamsin awoke to find herself lying in Ivo's large bed, his arm heavy across her waist, his dark head close to her own, his rugged features touchingly relaxed in sleep. She had no recollection of his carrying her up here last night, but she was inexpressibly moved that he'd placed her in his bed, and not in her own.

To have awoken to find herself already separated from him would have been too abrupt, too cruel for her to bear. She needed to take her own sad, silent farewell from him before the time came to pin a carefee smile on her face and exit gracefully from his life.

Tamsin didn't know where she was going to get that carefree smile from, and so she cherished these precious moments while he slept on, moments when she could still pretend he was hers, and hers alone.

She lay without moving for some time, studying him with eyes that were misty with love, storing up memories of him that would have to last her a lifetime.

Heavens, how she loved him! She felt awash with love, swamped by it, but it was a love that could be expressed for only one night, and now that night was over. This morning she had to find a way of making it easy for him to leave her without any of those 'pangs of conscience' he so hated.

That, if nothing else, would be a true measure of how very much she loved him.

Tamsin sighed, knowing that the longer she lingered

close to his strong, comforting body, the harder it would be for her to leave him. Just a few moments more, she promised herself. Just a few. . .and then she would get up and go away and they could both behave as though last night hadn't happened.

That, surely would be the kindest way to stage their separation. Ivo wouldn't have to rack his brains to say nice things to her, perhaps even pretend he'd look her up some time. It was all part of the polite ritual of separating that civilised people felt obliged to go through after a night of love, and Tamsin didn't think she could bear that.

Not for her and Ivo. Much, much better that she summoned up that carefree smile and assured him that she, too, wanted the break to be quick, clean and final, just the way he liked it.

But oh, it was going to be so hard! To try to make it easier, she forced herself to remember some of the things he'd said, things that had hurt enough at the time, but which hurt so much more now. Things like 'once you've seen one body, you've seen them all'.

Tamsin winced, then told herself firmly that she was being silly. She'd fallen asleep knowing that what had been a once-in-a-lifetime experience for her was just another brief encounter for Ivo, and she shouldn't expect things to be different now that she'd woken up again.

She'd made all her choices last night; this morning was where she began to live with them. Not in a few moments more, but now! Carefully she eased her face closer to Ivo's, pressed a kiss as light as gossamer on a lock of hair that lay darkly across his forehead, and murmured, 'I love you, my darling. I'll always love you.'

She didn't know why she had to tell him that, she only knew that she did, and in a strange way she felt a little better once she'd actually said the words out loud. Then she felt a lot worse because Ivo stirred and she was horrified in case he'd heard her. 'I hate it when women fall in love with me,' he'd said. 'It only complicates things, and it's so unnecessary.'

She accepted that Ivo couldn't love her, but she desperately didn't want him to hate her.

To her relief, he turned over and slept on, and now that she didn't have his arm across her waist she already felt separated from him. Cast off...

Biting her lip in anguished concentration, she eased herself out of bed, denied herself the indulgence of one last look at him and crept silently from the room.

Half an hour later she was feeding the cats and working in the stables, feeling guilty about having kept the animals waiting, but she hadn't known until she'd got downstairs that she'd overslept. It was past ten o'clock, and the fact that Ivo was still sleeping worried her a little. He was normally up before she was, so he must have been even more tired than she'd been last night.

Funny that she should be worrying about a man whose only worry about her now would be that she'd try to hang on to him, Tamsin thought, trying to smile at the irony of it but failing abysmally.

Humour of any kind was something she wasn't responding to this morning, perhaps because the bridge was the first sight that had greeted her eyes when she'd come out of the house. It was well above water-level, and traffic was already using it.

The natural forces that had conspired to trap her and Ivo together were now tearing them apart. Tamsin's eyes closed in anguish, but whatever she regretted it wasn't the halcyon hours they'd spent in each other's arms.

To her, that was the most natural, most wonderful thing that had ever happened to her. She just had to make sure it remained wonderful, and that was by letting Ivo know she had no regrets, and parting from him with a smile on her face...the smile that she still didn't know how she would summon up.

She heard the car coming up the hill before she saw it, and a cold hand clutched at her heart. She knew instinctively that it was Sara Lawley, and that her isolation with Ivo was truly over. As she walked to the front of the house to greet her Tamsin wished passionately that she'd sneaked upstairs for one last look at Ivo, spinning out for as long as possible her belief that while he still slept he was still hers—but it was too late now.

She rounded the side of the house to see a sturdy, freckle-skinned girl of around her own age climbing out of a battered Fiat. She had an honest, dependable face, which split into a friendly grin the moment she caught sight of Tamsin.

'Hi,' she said cheerfully. 'You don't have to tell me you're Gemma's sister, the family resemblance is too distinct. Sorry you've been under siege up here. I suppose my arrival is something like the relief of Mafeking.'

Tamsin felt as though Sara's arrival was the beginning of the end of her life, but she forced herself to grin back and respond lightly, 'Oh, it hasn't been so bad. Come in and I'll make you a cup of tea.'

'No, don't bother. Just introduce me to the animals, gen me up on the routine, and you can be on your way. Gemma told me you're a writer and were in the middle of something frightfully important when you came up here to help her out. It was only supposed to be for twenty-four hours, too, wasn't it? I bet you're hopping mad.'

'No, not mad, just a bit—delayed,' Tamsin replied carefully, leading the way back round the side of the house to the stables.

'But to be cut off, all alone, and you not used to this sort of work!' Sara exclaimed.

'Well, I'm certainly used to animals, and I haven't exactly been alone,' Tamsin replied, even more carefully. 'Mrs Durand's son arrived just before the bridge was flooded, and jolly useful he was as well when it came to coping with storm damage.'

That's struck just about the right note, she thought. She'd managed to make Ivo sound unremarkable instead of the most remarkable man who'd ever happened to her.

Sara's eyes widened. 'Gemma thought you were stuck here all by yourself.'

'I must have forgotten to mention him. I had a lot of other things on my mind at the time,' Tamsin responded airily. 'He'll be leaving today, anyway. He's going up to Cumberland to see his mother before he has to go abroad again. I hope you don't mind being on your own in a place as isolated as this.'

'I'll love it,' Sara replied. 'Lots of time for sketching and painting! I was a fine-arts student, you know, but I couldn't get a job when I left college. I joined Gemma's agency because it supports me while I paint my watercolours. Believe it or not, I'm actually beginning to sell a few!'

'That's super,' Tamsin enthused, relieved that the conversation had turned away from Ivo, and keeping it away from him while she introduced Sara to the animals and their routine.

Half an hour later she left Sara familiarising herself with the kitchen, retrieved her nightclothes from the parlour and went up to finish her packing. She tidied her room automatically, wholly obsessed with Ivo sleeping along the passage, and wondering how on earth she was going to manage parting from him.

But it was so strange, Ivo still in bed at this hour. With a heart like stone, Tamsin suddenly realised why: he didn't want the complication of saying goodbye to her. He was deliberately staying in bed until she'd left.

That, to her, an idealistic Aquarian, was the coward's way out—but, to a free-wheeling, free-loving Gemini, it might seem a quicker, cleaner, and probably even kinder way.

Tamsin beat down the urge to burst into tears, picked up her bags and went downstairs. Sara was making tea in the kitchen and she said in her friendly way, 'Like a cup before you set off on your travels?'

'No, I won't hang around. I've a lot of things to catch up on. You don't mind if I leave you to introduce yourself to Ivo, do you?'

'Of course not, but that's an unusual name—Ivo,' Sara replied, pouring hot water into the teapot. 'Hey, Ivo Durand! That couldn't be——?'

Tamsin tried to appear unconcerned. 'The society photographer? Yes, as a matter of fact, it is.'

'Golly! Half your luck being marooned here with him! And what do I get—the horses! What's he like?'

'You can make up your own mind about him when you meet him,' Tamsin replied, carefully avoiding Sara's big, eager eyes. 'I'm always too preoccupied when I'm writing a story to notice much about what's going on around me. I really do need to cut and run now, if you think you can cope.'

'Sure thing,' Sara replied. 'Have a safe journey.'

'Thanks.' Tamsin gave one last look around the kitchen, seeing things that Sara couldn't see—little vignettes of herself and Ivo, but mostly of Ivo. Ivo with his hair waving damply on his forehead, Ivo smiling, Ivo frowning, Ivo darkly flushed with passion. . .

He was everywhere she looked, and she knew he always would be.

He would forget her, but she would always be joined to him by the invisible thread of love her story had been about—the thread that would be her punishment and her reward for loving unwisely but completely for the first time in her life.

'Tamsin, are you all right?'

Sara's concerned voice came from out of nowhere, turning Tamsin's head towards her, although she had to wait for the mists of pain to clear before she could focus on her face. 'Me? Oh, I'm fine,' Tamsin bluffed vaguely. 'I was just looking round to make sure I haven't left anything behind.'

And I haven't, except my heart, she added to herself in silent anguish. That will always be here. With Ivo.

CHAPTER TEN

TAMSIN wrote her short story very fast, so fast that she suspected that it wrote itself. It was all about a reserved and emotionally fragile Aquarian girl who found herself marooned in an isolated house with a Gemini photographer whose light attitude to love was so very different from her own.

Her and Ivo.

But why not? He would never read it in the women's magazine that had commissioned it, and Tamsin hoped that by writing it she would somehow purge him from her mind.

She wrote it truly, as it had happened, including her quietly going away so that he would never know how deeply she'd fallen in love with him—deeply enough to let him go.

She shed tears over the story, hoped that was a sign that her fractured heart was healing, and called it *Love Came Suddenly*.

The fiction editor who'd commissioned it pulled a long face over the unhappy ending, and asked Tamsin to write in a glimmer of hope that the hero and heroine would be reunited eventually.

Tamsin argued passionately that there was no love truer than that which put somebody's happiness before one's own, but the editor was adamant—the ending had to be changed.

Tamsin took the story home, changed the title back to *The Thread of Love*, and shed more tears when she remembered that Ivo had thought it very poetical. Drying her eyes, she then wrote a very poetical ending about the thread of love that was supposed to link an Aquarian and a Gemini when they'd cared deeply about each other, a thread they could pull on when they needed to, no matter how much time had passed after they'd parted.

The fiction editor was delighted with the revision, but Tamsin sank into even deeper despair. She felt that writing about the thread of love was the one false thing about the story, because love itself prevented her from contacting Ivo again, and, left to himself, Ivo would never attempt to contact her.

She stopped crying simply because her tears had somehow become frozen in with the block of ice where her heart had once been. She retreated into her private world of make-believe, avoiding new relationships, letting old friendships slide, because then she didn't have to justify her long silences, her bleak eyes, her complete detachment from everything that was going on around her.

Her sister Gemma knew from Sara that Ivo had been at the house during the flood, but it was only when *The Thread of Love* was published several months later that Gemma put two and two together and made four.

'It's true, isn't it?' Gemma demanded. 'You've never written anything so passionately, so convincingly before.'

Her eyes were so full of sympathy that if Tamsin could she would have cried again. She hid her feelings, though, just as she had with Ivo. She told Gemma that yes, it was all true, but there was no need for compassion because she'd been very lucky to meet Ivo at a time when she hadn't been writing well.

'There's nothing like a new experience to get the inspiration flowing again,' she explained. 'In fact, an encounter with someone like Ivo once or twice a year and I'll be a best-selling author in no time at all.'

Her brittle gaiety worried Gemma so much that she went very quiet and asked no more questions, but Tamsin was aware of how often her thoughtful eyes dwelt on her and did her best to avoid them.

She knew that there would never be another Ivo for her, or anybody else, for that matter, but she was learning by degrees to live with the endless yearning that had become part and parcel of her daily life.

Well, perhaps live was too strong a word. She was learning to exist, and, if everything that was vital and joyous about her was trapped in a time capsule at an old flint and brick house on a hill in far-off Suffolk, then at least she was a richer person for having found out what it was like to truly love. So she told herself, and almost believed it.

She lost weight, weight she couldn't afford to lose, and when Gemma fretted about it Tamsin said it was because she was so very busy. Writing *The Thread of Love* might have failed to exorcise Ivo from heart and mind, but it had accelerated her already successful career.

Commissions came in so thick and fast that she scarcely had a moment to herself. At the grand old age of twenty-three she had, it seemed, loved enough and suffered enough to be able to transmit those emotions to her readers.

It was like winning a booby prize. The jackpot, she thought, belonged to whichever woman happened to be with Ivo right then. He would have been back in England a long time ago, of course. A full six months had passed since she'd lain in his arms.

She scoured all the newspapers and society magazines in the hope of gleaning some news of him, knowing she would be dreadfully hurt when she read his name coupled with another woman's, but for once he appeared to be living discreetly. Had he at last met a woman he could love enough to want to protect her from the harsh glare of publicity?

Tamsin crumbled inside at the thought, and actually whimpered, wondering despairingly whether the time would ever come when she could think of him without being stricken anew by the anguish eating into her soul.

Then at breakfast one Friday morning, Gemma looked over the newspaper she was reading and said, 'There's a new exhibition opening at the Dudleigh-Granville galleries on Monday.'

Tamsin carried on searching the gossip items in her paper and answered absently, 'What's special about that?'

'It's an exhibition of wildlife photographs by Ivo Durand.'

For a few seconds it seemed to Tamsin that time itself was suspended, then she became conscious of two things: one, that her heart was racing as it hadn't raced in months, and two, that Gemma's wide blue eyes were fixed unwaveringly on her.

'Should be worth a visit,' she managed to answer in the same absent tone. 'He's an excellent photographer.'

'I'm surprised he didn't send you a ticket for the opening day. He could have mailed it care of me. His mother knows the address of my agency.'

Tamsin had been painfully conscious for months that if Ivo had wanted to get in touch with her he could have done, but to reassure Gemma she replied, 'Didn't I tell you it was a no-strings-attached affair, and that we both wanted a quick, clean—and final—break?'

'Yes, and I still think what I thought at the time, that it doesn't sound a bit like you. You're a slow burner, Tamsin. You need time to get to know a person really well before you'd even dream of getting yourself involved. Having an affair with a virtual stranger isn't a bit like you.'

'It wasn't an affair, it was a fling, and we all step out of character sometimes. That's what makes life fun,' Tamsin responded evasively.

'Is it fun that's making you as pale as a ghost and as thin as a reed?'

'No, that's work, and, now that we're on the horrid subject, you'll be late opening up the agency if you don't get a move-on,' Tamsin replied blandly.

Gemma looked at her for a fulminating moment, then threw up her hands in despair. 'You were never an easy person to figure out, but I don't know you these days, I really don't. You've changed, and, however much you fob me off, I'm sure Ivo Durand is at the bottom of it.'

Tamsin didn't reply, and to her relief Gemma looked at her watch and pushed her chair back from the table. 'One of these days you and I are going to talk, my girl, really talk—but, in the meantime, you're right. I'm running late.'

She began hurrying around, collecting files and her handbag, while Tamsin sat on at the table, spreading marmalade on her toast and looking the picture of unconcern. The moment the front door slammed behind Gemma, though, she grabbed the newspaper her sister had discarded and read the advertisement about Ivo's exhibition with hungry eyes.

She had to see it, she knew she did, but not at the

opening on Monday. Ivo would be there. She didn't want to turn up like a ghost from pleasures past. No, he'd hate that sort of thing. So would she, if she had a big publishing launch and Simeon turned up to remind her of things she'd rather forget.

She'd let a few days go by until the novelty of the exhibition had worn off, then she'd creep quietly into the gallery, drink her fill of Ivo's work, feel closer to him, and creep away again. Next Friday would be just about right. Yes, she'd wait until then.

That weekend was the longest in Tamsin's memory, and all day Monday she had to more or less chain herself to her desk to stop herself from jumping into her car and racing to the gallery. She'd got used to her thoughts always being with Ivo, but now that she was within reaching distance of some kind of contact with him, however remote, it was so much worse.

There were items about the opening of his exhibition in Tuesday's newspapers. It seemed that everybody who was anybody had been there, and there were photographs of him. Tamsin studied them avidly, and thought that he must have been working too hard, because he looked strained and older than she remembered.

Yet all his dynamism and irresistible charisma still leapt out of his photographs as forcefully as they'd leapt out of the man himself on the night she'd first met him. Tamsin was seared with longing, almost destroyed by it, and it became harder still to stay away from the gallery.

No, she counselled herself frantically, I mustn't cave in now. I can hold out until Friday, just as I planned. I can, I can!

Late on Wednesday afternoon she surrendered, feeling she was being pulled to the gallery by forces she couldn't resist. It was April, the blooming of a new year. The old year had been close to dying when she'd parted from Ivo...

The weather was pretty much the same, though, a mixture of sunshine and rain, warm and chilly winds, and she deliberately dressed to look like a student so that she wouldn't call any attention to herself. Denim jacket and jeans, teamed with a navy blue sweater that did nothing for her too-pale face, and her hair tied firmly back.

There were quite a few people in the gallery, far more than she'd expected at this time in the afternoon, and, although she couldn't help resenting them because she wanted to be alone with Ivo's work—alone to think, to remember—she realised that, since anonymity was what she was after, it was much better to be one of a crowd.

She walked slowly from one photograph to the next, feeling close to Ivo, nearly as close as she did in her dreams. It was almost as though she'd spent the last six months drying up, turning inwards on herself, and now she was able to expand, even to live a little.

Surreptitiously she reached out and touched a photograph. It wasn't quite like touching Ivo, but it was the best she could hope for, and it helped her to lose herself in a world where there was love, not anguish; hope, not despair.

How long she was lost in that private world she didn't know, but she froze when a well-remembered and desperately loved voice said harshly, 'Still caring more passionately about causes than anything else, Tamsin?'

She turned slowly, so slowly that the whole world seemed to spin before her eyes before she found herself face to face with him. Tall, powerful, glowering at her with eyes that had haunted a thousand dreams, inspired a million tears. . .

'Did I say something like that?' she asked, trying to disguise the funny little catch in her voice. 'I can't remember. It all seems so long ago.'

It was a lie, of course. She remembered vividly every moment of her time with Ivo, every word they'd exchanged, every touch, intentional or accidental. It was the past six months that were a blur, a meaningless time that she'd somehow lived through, she had no idea how.

'You look dreadful,' he went on, barely concealed anger lashing out at her, an inexplicable anger that hurt her terribly and almost crushed what little spirit she had left. The world seemed to be spinning again, and she had to concentrate hard to hear him say, 'You're much too thin, much too pale.'

He made it sound like an accusation, but Tamsin was horrified that her appearance reflected how she was suffering because she loved him. She was frantic to cover her hurt, frantic to make him think all was well with her.

Somehow she managed to summon up a smile, and joked, 'So I look dreadful, do I? Thanks a million! I'll know who to look up the next time I need my ego stroked. I can only suppose that pressure of work is making me look a bit frayed around the edges. Not that I'm complaining! Success beats failure any time.'

'And now you know you're not a failure at anything, don't you?' he said between clenched teeth. 'I'm glad I had my uses.'

Tamsin caught her breath. He was alluding to her doubts about her sexuality, she was certain of it, but that was the last thing she'd expected him to refer to.

After all, he was the one who took his pleasures lightly, so lightly that he didn't want any comebacks.

And he hadn't had any from her. Tamsin wondered bewilderedly if she'd angered him by leaving him, instead of giving him the chance to leave her. No, surely not! His ego couldn't be that frail—not Ivo's!

She simply didn't know what to think, and was so afraid that her uncertainty would reveal just how vulnerable she was to his anger that she merely shrugged as though she wasn't interested enough to reply.

'Won't you at least admit that I had my uses?' he continued with a bitterness that came very close to hate.

Tamsin was so incapable of defending herself from an attack from him, especially an attack she didn't understand, that she was almost overcome, and had to turn sharply away to shield her face from him.

At that moment a crowd of people at the other end of the room spotted Ivo and surged towards him, waving their catalogues at him and calling for his autograph.

'Damn,' he swore. 'Tamsin, stay right where you are. Don't you dare move.'

But as soon as he was engulfed by the crowd Tamsin fled. Ivo had always been difficult to understand, but never so much as now when he seemed to resent her behaving exactly as he'd *wanted* her to behave.

It was so unjust, so unfair, like rubbing salt in wounds that had never healed, and she was so shattered that when she found herself in the busy street outside the gallery she walked straight past her car and kept on walking.

She was in no fit condition to drive, in no fit condition for anything as she walked blindly on, ricocheting off people hurrying homeward as the evening rush-hour began, being buffeted this way and that, but it was all nothing compared to the way she was being buffeted inside.

She'd imagined, deeply hoped, that if ever she and Ivo chanced to meet again it would be as friends—two people who had met briefly, loved briefly, parted amicably, and found at least a thread of something to join them—shared experience, something like that, since it couldn't be love.

It had been the last dream she'd had, the last dream she was ever likely to have, and now it was gone, blasted away by his unreasoning anger.

As she walked Tamsin forced herself to accept that it had always been a foolish dream, and there was no thread binding them, nor ever had been. All that had been wishful thinking, a last desperate bid to protect herself from the pain of knowing that everything between them had finished irrevocably the moment she'd quietly gone away to spare him the ritual of yet another farewell.

Obviously, she thought now, bitterness of her own beginning to well up through her anguish, Ivo had in some way felt cheated. But that wasn't her fault, it was his for staying in bed rather than facing her. How dared he blame her for it?

Her bitterness, however, was no protection against the devastation of realising they understood each other no better than they had the first night they'd met. She'd thought they'd overcome all that, but Ivo had just proved they were as much adversaries as they'd ever been. She couldn't bear that. She really couldn't.

Tamsin wasn't sure when her aimless wandering turned into a despairing need to get home—home, where there was safety, where she could close herself into her flat and give vent to all the despair and chagrin bottled up inside her.

When she reached the tall, graceful house in Kensington the agency was shut, as she had expected, but she was surprised to see there was a light on the second floor, which she and Gemma used as a communal living area and for entertaining friends.

She glanced at her watch and saw she'd been wandering for hours. It was past seven o'clock, but she'd thought Gemma was going straight out on a date after she'd closed the agency.

Obviously there'd been some sort of a hitch, and Tamsin didn't know how, under her sister's intelligent eyes, she was going to behave as normal, or as whatever passed for normal these days.

She was conscious of weariness as well as despair as she went up the stairs and into the big, comfortable sitting-room, but she fought it off and braced herself to smile. The smile froze on her lips as not Gemma, but Ivo rose from one of the deep armchairs. Tall, powerful, and infinitely threatening Ivo.

'Where the hell have you been?' he asked roughly.

Tamsin could only stand and stare at him, her soft lips trembling, all the vestiges of self-control she'd built up for Gemma's sake being stripped away by Ivo's penetrating eyes.

'You!' she managed shakily. 'Wh-what are you doing here?'

'What the blazes do you think?' he demanded, striding purposefully towards her.

Tamsin knew she couldn't take any more, but before she could turn to run Ivo grasped her shoulders and shook her mercilessly. 'I should wring your neck,' he ground out. 'The lord knows, you deserve it.'

'D-don't,' she managed to stutter. 'Please, Ivo, don't be angry with me any more. I only tried to do what you wanted.'

'Silly little fool,' he thundered, sweeping her into his arms. 'Do you know what hell you've put me through? *Six months* of absolute hell!'

He thrust her head savagely into his shoulder and held it there with a fierceness that robbed her of breath and reason. 'Don't you ever, *ever* walk out on me again. Do you hear me?' he thundered.

'Y-yes,' Tamsin gasped, 'b-but you. . .you didn't want me, not for keeps, and I only tried to make it easy for you.'

'That's why you're such a fool, almost as big a fool as I am,' he continued with such self-loathing that Tamsin fought her face free of his shoulder, looked up at him and shook her head in mute denial of his words.

He looked deep into her wide, distressed eyes, and by slow degrees the madness faded from his. He went on more quietly, 'I thought you used me to prove something to yourself. And, having proved it, you went away because you didn't need me any more. Do you know how much I hated you for that? How much I've suffered? How often I've nearly broken and returned to beg you to come back to me?'

Tamsin stared at him, unable to comprehend what he was saying to her. 'You didn't want any involvement,' she managed at last. 'That's what you told me . . .what I was trying to save you from.'

'That's what you told me, too, and what I've been going mad trying to save *you* from,' he told her, anger flaring again. 'We've wasted six precious months, and you're going to spend the rest of your life making up for it, I swear it.'

Something deep within Tamsin—hope, perhaps—was beginning to stir, even to sing, but she was afraid to let herself believe it. She said uncertainly, 'That night we made love, Ivo, do you remember?'

'Remember?' he exclaimed irascibly, 'I'm out of my mind through trying to forget it! Have you any idea what it was like to wake up to find you gone? No, of course you haven't,' he added violently, 'so I'll tell you. It was like being used and rejected. It wasn't so bad when I hated you for it, but the hate didn't last, only the pain. . .'

'Ivo. . .' Tamsin whispered, aghast. 'I thought I was the only one hurting. I thought you didn't want the. . . complication of seeing me again, and so—and so I left.'

'And broke my heart in doing it,' he accused.

'I didn't think you had a heart to be broken,' Tamsin pointed out with a flash of spirit. 'You never acted as though you had, not ever.'

'Not even when we made love?' he demanded.

'I thought that was just physical,' she faltered.

'Tamsin, no people in a merely physical relationship are ever the way we were.'

The way we were. . . Tamsin was so choked that she couldn't speak.

Ivo took advantage of her silence to say, 'I think I really will have to wring your neck, or——' and her pulses raced as his voice deepened '—kiss you.'

'Don't you dare,' she replied with a flicker of defiance. 'At the gallery this afternoon you acted as though you loathed me. I couldn't cope with that. It was so unfair.'

'So you ran away for the second time—and that, my love, is the last chance you'll ever get,' he told her. 'I've haunted that damned gallery hoping you'd show up, hoping you'd had enough freedom to be sick of it, hoping even more that that damned thread of love you were talking about would bring you back to me.'

He hesitated, then continued strangely brokenly, 'Monday, Tuesday, Wednesday...waiting, eternally waiting. Then when I finally saw you I never said a thing I meant to say, but all the things I shouldn't have. It's that cursed temper of mine. I'm so sorry, my darling, so truly sorry, but it slayed me, the way you didn't seem to care.'

'Not care...' she began.

Ivo gave her another little shake. 'Ssh,' he said, 'I haven't finished yet. That night we made love I wanted to tell you how much I loved you, but you fell asleep on me. I couldn't sleep for hours, thinking that, with my past, I might not be able to convince you I really loved you. I was so afraid of losing you. I didn't wake up the next morning because I was exhausted—not to avoid seeing you again. I never got a chance to tell you I loved you. I thought you'd guessed, and had run away because you didn't love me. I thought you'd just wanted to prove you weren't frigid, and, having proved it, still didn't want to get involved.'

He broke off, then ended raggedly, 'All I was left with were the photographs I'd taken of you.'

'The photographs you only took because you were bored!' Tamsin exclaimed.

'The photographs I took because I was already in love with you...a girl who had nothing but contempt for me, a girl I was frightened of even touching for fear of proving all the worst things she thought about me, a girl I didn't know how to win because I was too terrified of losing her. You, my darling.'

Tamsin could scarcely believe what she was hearing,

but her heart believed it. The hard knot of tears iced within her for so long began to melt. 'Ivo——'

'Will you be quiet?' he interrupted, but so tenderly that she thrust her head back into his shoulder, and shut her eyes tightly to hold back her tears. Now wasn't the time.

'That's better,' he went on. 'I haven't finished yet. I know I should be begging you to forget about my past and judge me only on how I am now, and how I will be in the future, but I can't afford to risk losing you again. So I'm ordering you to carry on loving me, if you possibly can, my darling.'

'C-carry on,' Tamsin stuttered. 'How do you know that I do?'

'When you vanished from the gallery I came straight here. Your sister let me in. She knows about us, doesn't she?'

'What do you mean, knows?' Tamsin asked cautiously.

'All there is to know. We talked, and when I'd convinced her that I wasn't—as she put it—after another fling she gave me a copy of the story you wrote about an Aquarian girl and a Gemini man. Not David and Maria, Tamsin, but us. I understood everything then, but most of all I understood what a truly wonderful girl I'd fallen in love with. It's taken me a long time, but I was waiting for the best.'

Tamsin's lips trembled. She compressed them, then asked, 'Then why have you stayed away from me for so long?'

'I thought if I found you again, if I tried to hold on to you, I'd make you as unhappy as Simeon did. I couldn't do that, not the way I loved you, will always love you.'

'Ivo,' Tamsin whispered, awed, 'you—you weren't trying to be *noble*, were you?'

'Yes,' he said savagely, 'and I can promise you I'll never be noble again, not after nearly losing you because of it.'

'Oh, Ivo!' Tamsin choked and bent her head as her tears welled in her eyes and spilled helplessly down her cheeks. 'No, don't—please, don't ever be noble. That's only for dreams...and...and I don't need dreams now.'

And she didn't, she realised with wonder. All she needed was Ivo, big, brutal, tender, loving, wonderful Ivo.

'You're crying,' he said, turning her face up to his and studying her with alarm. 'Don't cry, my love.'

'No, of course not,' she replied. 'I k-know a Gemini man can't cope with tears.'

'What a Gemini man can't cope with is an Aquarian girl who hides her feelings from him, then has the nerve to write a story that tells the whole world about it,' he retorted, wiping her tears tenderly away.

'It wasn't an exposé,' she said quickly. 'I wouldn't want you to think——'

'I don't,' he interrupted her. 'It was a love-story, and, since it will soon be common knowledge that it's *our* love-story, will you at least salvage my reputation by marrying me?'

'I suppose I'll have to,' Tamsin responded, smiling mistily up at him. 'After all, only a silly, misguided little fool would ever think of doing anything so foolish.'

'You'll never regret it,' he promised with a resurgence of his old arrogance. 'Never, ever, I swear it.'

'I know,' Tamsin whispered, 'but if you ever think I'm regretting it, all you have to do is tug on the thread of love that binds us, and I'll be at the end of it.'

'You won't be at the end of anything,' Ivo said roughly, 'you'll always be right with me. And when we're married we'll live in Suffolk in the house meant for the children that I'd never thought I'd have, because I never believed in love. Do you remember, Tamsin, that I said children need stability?'

'Yes,' she murmured breathlessly, remembering how bitter he'd been because his own father had left his family, a bitterness, she realised now, that had warped his whole life.

'Do you think we can give them that stability? I know I can—with you.'

'And I can—with you,' she whispered.

His arms tightened around her, his lips closed on hers, and he whispered against her lips, 'I love you, darling.'

'I love you, too,' Tamsin whispered back blissfully.

Ivo raised his head, looked teasingly into her eyes, and asked, 'How did it go? That bit about "David's feather-light kisses traced the line of her jaw and continued their sensuous journey of exploration downwards. . ."?'

'I forget,' Tamsin lied, her own eyes coming alive with laughter. 'Improvise.'

So Ivo did.

STARGAZING

YOUR STAR SIGN: AQUARIUS (January 21–February 19)

AQUARIUS is the third of the Air signs and is ruled by Uranus and Saturn. This is considered by many to be the sign of the future since the planet combinations result in a highly original character. As the Water Bearer, Aquarians may tend to show a rather cool nature towards others but, despite this, your bubbly nature means that you tend to make friends easily. However, others should beware since your highly individualistic nature may mean that you find your patience being tested when it comes to working closely with others.

Your characteristics in love: Aquarians tend to be rather wary of entering deep relationships although they often have many superficial ones. As a result, partners often need to display a great deal of patience. However, once an Aquarian has overcome his or her natural shyness and reserve, loved ones will be rewarded—an Aquarian in love is loyal, trusting and unlikely to deceive.

Star signs which are compatible with you: The signs of **Gemini, Libra, Sagittarius** and **Aries** all tend to be compatible with your cool ways while you may find that sparks fly if you choose partners with the characteristics of **Leo, Scorpio** or **Taurus**. Other signs may also be compatible depending on which planets reside in their Houses of Personality and Romance.

What is your star-career? With their cool, logical ways, Aquarians tend to be brilliant at predicting trends and, while they tend not be particularly motivated by financial rewards, it is often they who receive them! Aquarians also tend to be highly intelligent which may well suit careers in such demanding jobs as computing, scientific research, ecology and—dare we say it—even astrology!

Your colours and birthstones: As your sign is ruled by Air, it is hardly surprising that your birthstones are aquaramine or amethyst, both of which reflect your concise, logical clear thinking. You tend to also prefer pale colours such as blue which have a calming influence in your naturally hectic life.

AQUARIUS ASTRO-FACTFILE

Day of the week: Wednesday
Countries: Sweden and Zimbabwe
Flowers: Orchids
Food: Rhubarb, beansprouts. Aquarians often tend to find that food is low on their list of priorities—they are often too full of wonderful ideas in their heads to be concerned with their stomachs!
Health: Aquarians, with their intelligence and naturally busy lives, occasionally find themselves to be out of touch with their bodies which can lead to exhaustion. Plenty of rest, relaxation and frequent changes of scenery are necessary to keep you in tip-top condition!

You share your star sign with these famous names:

Vanessa Redgrave
Paul Newman
John Hurt
Placido Domingo

Marti Caine
Barry Humphries
Ronald Reagan

Love is in the Air...

Mills & Boon have commissioned four of your favourite authors to write four tender romances.

Guaranteed love and excitement for St. Valentine's Day

A BRILLIANT DISGUISE	-	Rosalie Ash
FLOATING ON AIR	-	Angela Devine
THE PROPOSAL	-	Betty Neels
VIOLETS ARE BLUE	-	Jennifer Taylor

Available from January 1993   PRICE £3.99

Mills & Boon

Available from Boots, Martins, John Menzies, W.H. Smith, most supermarkets and other paperback stockists. Also available from Mills & Boon Reader Service, PO Box 236, Thornton Road, Croydon, Surrey CR9 3RU.

THE PERFECT GIFT FOR MOTHER'S DAY

Specially selected for you – four tender and heartwarming Romances written by popular authors.

LEGEND OF LOVE -
Melinda Cross

AN IMPERFECT AFFAIR -
Natalie Fox

LOVE IS THE KEY -
Mary Lyons

LOVE LIKE GOLD -
Valerie Parv

Mills & Boon

Available from February 1993   Price: £6.80

*Available from Boots, Martins, John Menzies, W.H. Smith, most supermarkets and other paperback stockists.
Also available from Mills & Boon Reader Service, PO Box 236, Thornton Road, Croydon, Surrey CR9 3RU.
(UK Postage & Packing free)*

Accept 4 FREE Romances and 2 FREE gifts

FROM READER SERVICE

An irresistible invitation from Mills & Boon Reader Service. Please accept our offer of 4 free Romances, a CUDDLY TEDDY and a special MYSTERY GIFT... Then, if you choose, go on to enjoy 6 captivating Romances every month for just £1.70 each, postage and packing free. Plus our FREE Newsletter with author news, competitions and much more.

**Send the coupon below to:
Reader Service, FREEPOST,
PO Box 236, Croydon,
Surrey CR9 9EL.**

--- NO STAMP REQUIRED ---

Yes! Please rush me 4 Free Romances and 2 free gifts! Please also reserve me a Reader Service Subscription. If I decide to subscribe I can look forward to receiving 6 brand new Romances each month for just £10.20, post and packing free.
If I choose not to subscribe I shall write to you within 10 days - I can keep the books and gifts whatever I decide. I may cancel or suspend my subscription at any time. I am over 18 years of age.

Ms/Mrs/Miss/Mr _____ EP30R

Address _____

_____

Postcode _____ Signature _____

Offer expires 31st May 1993. The right is reserved to refuse an application and change the terms of this offer. Readers overseas and in Eire please send for details. Southern Africa write to Book Services International Ltd, P.O. Box 42654, Craighall, Transvaal 2024.
You may be mailed with offers from other reputable companies as a result of this application. If you would prefer not to share in this opportunity, please tick box ☐

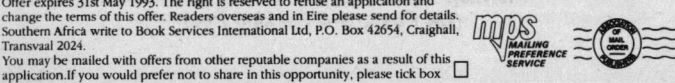

Next Month's Romances

Each month you can choose from a wide variety of romance with Mills & Boon. Below are the new titles to look out for next month, why not ask either Mills & Boon Reader Service or your Newsagent to reserve you a copy of the titles you want to buy — just tick the titles you would like and either post to Reader Service or take it to any Newsagent and ask them to order your books.

Please save me the following titles:	Please tick	√
AN OUTRAGEOUS PROPOSAL	Miranda Lee	
RICH AS SIN	Anne Mather	
ELUSIVE OBSESSION	Carole Mortimer	
AN OLD-FASHIONED GIRL	Betty Neels	
DIAMOND HEART	Susanne McCarthy	
DANCE WITH ME	Sophie Weston	
BY LOVE ALONE	Kathryn Ross	
ELEGANT BARBARIAN	Catherine Spencer	
FOOTPRINTS IN THE SAND	Anne Weale	
FAR HORIZONS	Yvonne Whittal	
HOSTILE INHERITANCE	Rosalie Ash	
THE WATERS OF EDEN	Joanna Neil	
FATEFUL DESIRE	Carol Gregor	
HIS COUSIN'S KEEPER	Miriam Macgregor	
SOMETHING WORTH FIGHTING FOR	Kristy McCallum	
LOVE'S UNEXPECTED TURN	Barbara McMahon	

If you would like to order these books in addition to your regular subscription from Mills & Boon Reader Service please send £1.70 per title to: Mills & Boon Reader Service, P.O. Box 236, Croydon, Surrey, CR9 3RU, quote your Subscriber No:............................
(If applicable) and complete the name and address details below. Alternatively, these books are available from many local Newsagents including W.H.Smith, J.Menzies, Martins and other paperback stockists from 12th February 1993.

Name:...
Address:..
....Post Code:........................

To Retailer: If you would like to stock M&B books please contact your regular book/magazine wholesaler for details.

You may be mailed with offers from other reputable companies as a result of this application.
If you would rather not take advantage of these opportunities please tick box ☐